My Jesus And Prohibition

What Would Jesus Do?

by
Texas Nathan
texas_nathan83@yahoo.com

Ὑπό Τῷ Ἡλιῷ

HYPO TO HELIO BOOKS

Houston

BISAC Subject Headings:
Fic014000—Fiction > Historical
Fic042030—Fiction > Christian > Historical
His036060—History > United States > 20th Century
His036130—History > United States > State & Local > Southwest (AZ, NM, OK, TX)
Rel012120—Religion > Christian Life > Spiritual Growth

HYPO TO HELIO BOOKS, 2427 Clearbrook Dr., Missouri City, TX, 77489-6061

"Sheriff Don" in "Copperas County" is *not* based on Walter Warren Hollingsworth, Coryell County sheriff between 1914 and 1934.

Morris Sheppard, who is mentioned in this story, was a real person. He was a United States senator from Texas who was fervently prohibitionist. His cousin's son Richard Sheppard, however, is fictional.

In Chapter 11, speechmaker Elimelech Marshall is a plagiarist. Or perhaps I the author am. Marshall's speech takes quotes from the Anti-Saloon League of New York, William Jennings Bryan, and Billy Sunday.

This story contains adult language and situations. It is not suitable for Christian teenagers.

PART 1
Prohibition In
Theory, 1917

The right of prohibition is inherent in all law, human and divine. "Thou shalt not" is repeated more than ten times in the Decalogue. "Thou shalt not" prefaced the test law of Eden, and that restriction had reference to the indulgence of the appetite. The model law of the holy people had many clauses which would be objected to now as sumptuary laws. But such prohibitions do not interfere with individual liberty, for that implies only the freedom to do right; while the freedom to do wrong in not liberty but license.

—Prohibition tract, 1880s

Chapter 1
What Would Jesus Do?

Sunday morning, March 18, 1917

Ellen Frost felt glorious, and she felt awful. *Lord Jesus, my spirit burns with joy and guilt both*, she thought.

Ten feet in front of twenty-year-old Ellen, Brother Bob Garner was preaching: "What would Jesus do? This is the only question for Christians: What would Jesus do?"

Ellen wanted to weep for the beauty of Brother Bob's message, a message as holy as a burning bush—

And yet what the message was saying was that Ellen was only a costume-store Christian. Sitting in the pew, Bible in her lap, parents to her right, Ellen felt ashamed.

What would Jesus do about Danny Payne? Ellen wondered. Jesus made no answer.

"Tateville," Brother Bob continued, "is a small town like Nazareth; Texas in summer is hot like Israel. Jesus understands what our life is like."

Brother Bob isn't usually so full of the Holy Ghost, Ellen thought in passing. Usually when Brother Bob preached sin, it was the sins of Tateville's coloreds and white trash that he denounced.

<<It's sure easier to think about Brother Bob's faults than your own, hmm?>> the Tempter said to Ellen. Ellen imagined the Tempter standing by the end of the pew, wearing a natty burgundy-colored suit and giving her a smirk. For some reason, whenever Ellen pictured the Tempter, he had the face and body of her cousin Johnny.

"But did Jesus follow the crowd?" Brother Bob asked Ellen. Brother Bob was looking at all the Baptists, but Ellen knew that his words were meant for her alone. "Did others tell Jesus what was behaving good enough?"

<<These fine, respectable people think Ellen Frost is good enough,>> the Tempter said. He belly-laughed. <<Good, *you?* I know your secret wish.>>

I also wish to please my Savior, Ellen told the Tempter.

****

"No, Jesus wasn't a sheep, He led the sheep," Brother Bob said, answering his own question.

Audrey Frost leaned over. "That handsome man is looking at you," she murmured.

It took Ellen a second to realize what her mother meant: *First Baptist has a new marriage prospect, and he maybe wants to court you.*

Any other Sunday, this would have been exciting news, and Ellen would have spent the rest of the service eye-flirting with him—

<<In a good Christian way, of course,>> the Tempter pointed out, <<as you both miss the sermon in the process.>>

—But at the moment, men and boys were a distraction from Jesus. Ellen gave Audrey a smile and murmured back, "I love you, Mommy, please hush." Ellen didn't give her mystery admirer so much as a glance.

****

The choir director was eyeing Brother Bob from behind, waiting for his cue.

"Jesus was God, but also a man," Brother Bob said, "and He showed how God wants Man to live. If you do not know Jesus, do you see that you are a sinner, thus condemned to hell?"

"Amen, Brother Bob," Ellen said. Audrey, puzzled, glanced at Ellen.

Brother Bob said, "Come forward and accept Jesus into your heart."

<<I hate this part,>> said the Tempter.

Brother Bob continued, "Christian, come rededicate yourself to live as Jesus lived, and love as Jesus loved."

A second spiritual voice spoke now, in gentle tones: ++Come, Ellen. Taste again the joys of perfect obedience.++

<<`Perfect obedience,' my ass,>> the Tempter said, laughing. <<Ellen won't obey You, not with the way she hates Danny Payne.>>

****

Brother Bob continued: "Christian, come rededicate yourself to live as Jesus lived, and love as Jesus loved."

"Oh, I will, I will," Ellen said.

<<We'll see,>> snickered the Tempter.

Brother Bob made a hand gesture, and the choir director raised his baton. Brother Bob continued, "As we sing hymn number 184, I invite those who need to, to step forward. Now—don't wait."

Ellen stood (which surprised her mother anew), straightened her shoulders, moved to the aisle, and made a beeline for Brother Bob.

The Tempter wasn't physically in the aisle, of course, so he couldn't block her way. But Ellen heard his mocking voice: <<You can't make this work, and you know it.>>

Get thee behind me, snake-breath, Ellen shot back.

Seconds later, Ellen was standing by Brother Bob.

****

As soon as the Invitation hymn began, Richard Sheppard saw the quarry stand up and make straight for the preacher. So Richard also stood and also went to see the preacher. Richard gave the girl a smile to endanger hymens—and Sweetheart there didn't even notice.

Richard thought, *Damn, what do I have to do to make her notice me?*

From boyhood, Richard had bagged the most beautiful girls, the girls whom ugly boys desired but could never have. And this woman who stood on the preacher's other side had beauty to spare: a trim figure, flawless skin, pale green eyes in a sculpted face, and long chestnut hair that shone like a floozy's cheap jewelry. This woman was definitely up to Richard's standards.

So why had he not caught her eye in an hour of trying? Was she one of those *unnatural* women? Perhaps she, like Richard, needed the cloak of respectability that a Baptist church provided.

Well, if this brunette stunner were a lesbian, Richard would relish the challenge of seducing her. It had been a long time since he'd found any challenge in seduction.

****

The choir and congregation were singing the hymn as Ellen and Brother Bob stood at the front of the church.

Softly and tenderly Jesus is calling,
Calling for you and for me,
See on the portals He's waiting and watching,
Watching for you and for me.
Come home, come home,
Ye who are weary, come home,
Earnestly, tenderly, Jesus is calling,
Calling, O sinner, come home!

Old Mrs. Carter and, next to her, the Widow Manx each were eyeing Ellen over their hymnals. *What are you feeling guilty about, girl?* their looks said.

Brother Bob was looking at Ellen, perhaps wondering the same thing. So she said, "Brother Bob, I want to live by `What would Jesus do.' "

"Sister Ellen, that's wonderful," he said with practiced enthusiasm.

"After the service, could you go through the Bible, give me more tips what Jesus would do?"

For an instant, his eyes told Ellen, *I don't want to.*

But quickly his eyes and face changed to match his smooth voice: "Sister Ellen, I'd love to. But we're going to hear a special speaker after the service."

Brother Bob nodded toward a gorgeous blond man, then said to Ellen, "Excuse me, but someone else is waiting."

Brother Bob turned toward the stranger, but then Ellen touched the preacher's arm. She asked, "When I do what Jesus would do, God will take away my burden?"

Brother Bob turned back to Ellen, and his eyes held surprise. "You have a burden?"

****

Three minutes later, Brother Bob made another hand gesture, and the music director quieted the choir. Ellen stood at Brother Bob's right, and the stranger to Brother Bob's left, all three facing the congregation. Brother Bob spoke into the silence.

"Ellen Frost comes forward to rededicate her life to Jesus. Richard Sheppard comes on promise of letter from Calvary Baptist Church of Paris, Texas. All those who welcome them and the decisions they've made today, say `Amen!' "

"*Amen!*"

As Brother Bob led the closing prayer, the stranger Richard smiled at Ellen. Ellen's smile back was warm as she thought, *Oh my, the Lord provides!* Had God rewarded her obedience by quickly providing her with the perfect husband?

With the service ended, well-wishers were moving forward to shake the hands of Ellen and newcomer Richard. Before the congregation could reach the young people, Ellen turned to Richard. "Are you staying for the fellowship picnic?" she asked, trying to sound sisterly.

Richard answered her with a handsome smile, then said, "*Now* I am."

Chapter 2
Jabez Doesn't Pray

Ten minutes later
Lawn outside First Baptist Church, Tateville

The picnic was being held on the grounds of the church. Near the serving tables were two ice chests, with ice picks within reach. People were sitting on blankets on the grass.

Waiting in line to take food were Richard, Ellen, Ellen's parents John and Audrey, and Ellen's aunt and uncle, Agatha and Horace.

While John and Audrey were caring folk, Aunt Agatha and Uncle Horace could try the soul, some days. Ellen hoped that this would not be one of those days.

Richard asked, "So what's to do in this town?"

Ellen said, "Tateville has two flicker theaters, and both have organists."

Mommy sidled up to Ellen and murmured, "Ellie, was there anything you want to tell me?"

Ellen said carefully, "What do you mean, Mommy?"

"You went forward today. Something bothering you?"

Ellen said, "If there was, Mommy, Brother Bob's sermon shows me the way out."

A man stepped out of his automobile then, and walked onto the church's lawn. The newcomer was wearing a clerical collar, which marked him instantly as no Baptist. Brother Bob walked over to the new arrival and spoke a few words as he shook the man's hand.

****

Meanwhile, in a Dallas brothel

The owner of the brothel, Jabez McDaniel, was holding open the door for, and smiling at, a fat man who was leaving. Very much unlike the customer, Jabez had an athletic look and was sharply dressed. Jabez was charming when it suited his purposes.

The two-story brothel had a first-floor lobby, cheaply furnished. On both the first and second floors was a central hallway going to the back. Facing the lobby (on the first floor), the stairs and railing (on the second floor), and each central hallway from either side, were many doors. Each door showed a room number.

In a corner of the lobby was the cashier's cage. Standing outside the cashier's cage was an armed guard. Beyond the lobby, the first-floor rooms had an ogreish bouncer sitting nearby.

Sitting in a chair at the top of the stairs was the second-floor bouncer, Joe Winthrop.

Joe was one mean-looking character. Which was why Jabez had hired him: Joe was there to make men customers behave and to scare the daylights out of the women.

A different fat man came to the head of the stairs, holding a slip of paper in his hand. He looked unhappy as he called down to Jabez. "Mr. McDaniel?"

Jabez said, "Please, call me Jabez."

"She told me to get out. Said I was too fat."

Jabez said (while rushing up the stairs), "She did, did she?"

Jabez was now next to the customer. Jabez glanced at the slip of paper in the other man's pudgy hand.

Handwritten on the paper was the number *15*.

Jabez said, "Annabelle's gotten uppity? Sir, why don't you wait downstairs."

****

Jabez rushed to Room 15. Then he shoved in the door. "You dirty, worthless, pile of shit. What the hell do you think you're doing?"

Inside was "Annabelle," a gaunt young long-haired blonde with a Texas accent. Jabez didn't remember her original name (and didn't care). When the girl had been "recruited," she had looked like she could be Mary Pickford's twin. Of course, the resemblance had been stronger before the girl in Room 15 had lost all the weight.

Now Annabelle cowered on the bare mattress of the bed. She wore lingerie and a neck ring. A small padlock attached the neck ring to chain.

The other end of the chain was padlock-looped around a bedpost of the metal bed. The chain was long enough that she could reach the sink, with its pitcher, mirror, and cosmetics; and she could sit on the chamber pot. But she couldn't walk out the door.

Annabelle said, "The last man was fat too. I can't breathe when fat pigs lie on me."

Jabez advanced on her and backhanded/slapped her, two quick hits. He was about to slap her again, but she ran away. He yanked the chain; she fell, choking, onto her butt. He rolled her onto her stomach and jerked her arm back, hurting her.

Annabelle said, "*Please.*"

Jabez said, "`Please' what? `Please let me fuck that man like I mean it'?"

Annabelle said, "God, I hate you."

Jabez pulled harder on her arm.

Jabez said, "I don't give a dead rat, so long you do what I tell you."

Annabelle said, "All right, damn you."

****

Seconds later

Jabez was standing in the hallway outside Room 15. He had the room's door open.

Jabez said, "Pull shit like this again, and no dope for forty-eight hours."

Jabez strode to the stairs.

Joe asked, "Hey boss, you really gonna cut off Annabelle's heroin?"

Jabez said, "Hell no, who wants a whore who throws up? But my hop-fiend harem was more scared of going off junk than of a beating."

Jabez came downstairs. He gave the fat man a smile and walked him upstairs to Room 15—

The fat man said, "I appreciate it, Mr. McDaniel."

Jabez said, "Please, call me Jabez."

"Not sure I can remember it. Never heard that name before."

Jabez said, "It's in the Bible, means `pain of childbirth.' Always a hoot, my ma."

****

Meanwhile, at the Baptist Church picnic

Richard, Ellen, and her relatives now had full plates of food, and were sitting on a blanket and eating.

Ellen noticed that Brother Bob finished speaking to the man wearing the clerical collar. Brother Bob stepped forward.

Brother Bob said, "Everyone, your attention please? The Reverend Odysseus Covington had a message all Christians who love our country must hear."

Dad sighed, then he said, "Here we go again—another speech about the evils of drink."

Mommy, eyeing the crowd, said, "Ssh!"

Odysseus clearly burned with zeal as he stepped forward. "Good Christians, I am here on behalf of the Anti-Saloon League of Texas. I come to warn you of the evils of intoxicating drink."

As Odysseus began to speak, a horse-drawn wagon pulled up, Franklin's Ice. The driver, Franklin, was a colored man whose face told Ellen that he'd lived a hard life.

From the wagon Franklin, brought two big blocks of ice, which he carried to the church-picnic ice chests. Church men begin immediately to hack at the ice with ice picks.

While Odysseus orated to the crowd and Franklin delivered ice, the six people on the blanket talked:

Uncle Horace asked Richard, "Are you any relation to Senator Sheppard?"

Richard glanced at Ellen for some reason. Then he said, "Yes sir, Morris Sheppard is my father's first cousin."

Ellen said nothing, but was impressed.

Odysseus said to the crowd, "What is God's view of intoxication? Samson, Samuel, Daniel, and John the Baptist were all total abstainers."

His ice delivered, Franklin went to Brother Bob to get paid. But Brother Bob was talking to a church member (while trying to eat), so Franklin had to wait.

Aunt Agatha said to Ellen, "You went forward today."

Ellen said, "Yes, Aunt Agatha, to live like Jesus lived."

Aunt Agatha said, "But now people will wonder what you feel guilty about."

Tense Ellen asked, "Why does everyone keep asking me that?"

****

Then Ellen started dreaming. Except that she was wide awake.

Or maybe she was *day*dreaming. But this "daydream" wasn't pleasant.

Or maybe Ellen was having a vision. But only people in the Bible got visions, right?

Anyway, while a small part of Ellen's mind was paying attention to what was being said around her, the biggest part of Ellen's mind was watching a movie in her head. Except that this movie wasn't in black-and-white, it was in full color.

In the movie, or vision, or daydream, Ellen and Jesus were outside of Frost's Hardware And Lumber, walking along the sidewalk. Ellen carried a black purse and a loaf of bread.

Uncle Horace asked Richard, "Think your senator uncle will declare war against Germany?"

Sitting on the sidewalk was a colored beggar girl, aged between ten and twelve, and dressed shabby. Near her was a hat (with only a few coins) and a worn pair of crutches.

The Negro beggar girl held her hand out as Jesus and Ellen passed.

Richard replied, "If President Wilson asks him to."

Jesus stopped Ellen with a gesture. Jesus took Ellen's bread, broke it in half, and gave a half-loaf to the child.

Ellen started to walk on, but Jesus looked at her with a raised eyebrow and a smile. Ellen put her own half-loaf in the girl's hat.

Ellen started to walk away again, but again Jesus gave her an eyebrow and a smile, as He eyed her purse. Catching His meaning, Ellen opened her purse.

Odysseus proclaimed, "At the Last Supper, our Lord called the liquid they drank `the fruit of the vine,' and Paul referred to `the Cup' of Communion. Intoxicating wine was never mentioned."

In Ellen's purse was a five-dollar bill and a revolver. Holding the purse so that Jesus couldn't see the gun, she took the money out and quickly closed the purse.

Ellen put the money into the beggar-girl's hat. Jesus gave Ellen a smile, but then His gaze dipped to her purse, and Jesus turned sad.

****

Uncle Horace said, "Wilson, humph. He promised to keep our sons out of war."

Now Ellen of the picnic was watching herself star in another vision-movie. But this time, Ellen and Jesus were in a prison hospital.

Movie-Ellen—carrying the same purse as before—and Jesus walked down the prison hospital's central hallway.

Visible were bustling doctors and nurses, and a nurses' station; but also could be seen a barred door attended by two prison guards. A convict walked down the hallway, handcuffed to a guard; the convict's "free" arm was in a sling. A second convict moved himself in a wheelchair.

Ellen was walking past one patient-room when Jesus's gesture stopped her. Holding her gaze, He turned and walked into the room. Visible in the room was a convict in bandages.

Dad said, "Be fair, Horace. Blame those U-boat captains, not Wilson."

Ellen was about to follow Jesus into the room when the Man walked out into the hallway. Neither Ellen nor Jesus could see the Man's face, but Ellen recognized the Man. *Why is he here?* Ellen thought. She felt shock, fear, then anger.

Ellen's hands went to her purse, as she prepared to follow the Man.

But in the patient-room, Jesus held His hand out and His eyebrow up, and He was smiling: *Come.*

Ellen went to Jesus, took His hand, and let herself be pulled into the room—but her eyes were still on the Man's retreating back. Her free hand played with the clasp of her purse, eager to grasp the pistol that waited inside.

****

Odysseus proclaimed, "What did Jesus turn water into, at the wedding at Cana? Was it wine? Folks, the word used was `oinos.' `Oinos' can be translated as `grape juice.' "

Now Ellen of the picnic watched Ellen and Jesus in a third vision-movie. This time Ellen of the movie was just outside that never-to-be-forgotten room at the Bluebonnet Hotel, at night. Movie-Ellen still held the same black purse.

The hotel room had 1916 decoration, with a bed, a fan rotating over that bed, a nightstand by the bed, and a chair by the window. On the nightstand was a brown-glass medicine bottle and a castoff men's handkerchief.

Jesus walked into the room, Ellen following. Seeing this room gave movie-Ellen a moment of panic. She picked up the bottle and was staring at its label when Jesus gestured: *Look.*

Dad said, "Or that word can mean `wine.' "

Movie-Ellen discovered the Man standing by the hotel-room window and near the chair. The Man was facing Ellen and Jesus; he also was frozen in time, a naked statue. At the Man's bare feet was a silent-movie script.

Reluctantly Ellen put down the bottle. It took Jesus much coaxing by gesture for Ellen even to come near the Man.

When both Jesus and Ellen were near, Jesus gave a long hug to the Man's unmoving form. Jesus stepped back, and His hand and eyebrow both give Ellen the message: *Your turn.*

Odysseus proclaimed, "What about when Paul advised Timothy, `Drink no longer water, but use a little wine for thy stomach's sake and for thine often infirmities'? Back then, people couldn't get pure water to drink."

Instead of hugging the Man, Ellen's heart filled with rage. Quickly she opened her purse, yanked out the revolver, and shot the Man many times.

****

Meanwhile, at the Baptist Church picnic

Now Ellen's hand pushed away her evil act of the daydream.

Ellen blurted out, "Anyway, I'm going to do what Jesus would do."

Mommy said, "I'm so proud of you."

Aunt Agatha said, "When you're sensible about it."

Ellen asked, "What do you mean by `sensible'?"

Uncle Horace said, "Jesus didn't smoke, He didn't gamble, He went to church every Sunday. You do all that, you're okay."

Aunt Agatha said, "Out there are evil men who bother pretty girls. Obey Jesus, but don't risk your virtue."

Ellen's answer was unexpectedly intense: "Yes, there are such men."

Then Ellen added, "But Jesus said to preach the gospel to every creature."

Aunt Agatha said, "We had missionaries for that."

Dad said, "My baby, now a fanatic. Oh well."

Ellen replied, "Religion's like hardware, Dad. You get what you pay for."

Odysseus proclaimed, "God calls us to rescue our brethren trapped by the bottle: `We that are strong ought to bear the infirmities of the weak,' Paul wrote."

Ellen said, "I wish Johnny could hear this man."

Richard asked casually, "Who's Johnny?"

Odysseus proclaimed, "Intoxicating drink is a poison, it impoverishes families, it ruins the reputation of women, and it causes industrial accidents and motorcar accidents. I cannot say one good thing about intoxicating drink."

A man in the crowd said, "Amen." Dad frowned.

Ellen explained to Richard, "Johnny's my first cousin. He's a sweetie, and he's cute too. He owns a traveling medicine show."

Richard raised an eyebrow, but Ellen couldn't guess why. After all, she wasn't describing a dreamy silent-screen hero, she was describing her cousin.

Uncle Horace said, "A traveling medicine show is no fit profession for a Christian."

Richard said, "Anyway, Johnny isn't your beau."

Ellen said, "He's my cousin. But I wouldn't mind someone like him as my beau."

Ellen hoped Richard would take her hint.

Odysseus asked, "Good Christians, will you stand idle while strong drink destroys your fellow Americans?"

Several men and women in the audience answered "No!"

Dad asked, "Is anyone beside me listening to this blowhard?"

Ellen said, "Brother Bob wouldn't have invited him if this were false teaching."

Franklin the ice man finally had been paid, and was headed back to his wagon. Ellen waved to him.

Ellen said, "Bye, Franklin. Give your life to Jesus—let Him wash away your sins."

Franklin looked around at the other faces there (all white, unlike his own), then he scowled as he looked back at Ellen. "Miss Frost, I knows lots more about sin than you does."

Ellen was stung by the putdown. Meanwhile, Franklin climbed onto the driver's seat of his wagon and drove his team away.

Odysseus proclaimed, "Now, intoxicants had been outlawed here in Copperas County for three years. And last week their sale was outlawed in Washington, D.C."

Uncle Horace said, "Colored folks don't respect God's Sabbath, or God's message. Tsk."

Dad said, "We asked for ice. Was it going to walk here by itself?"

Aunt Agatha asked, "Why did you talk to him, anyway? A good girl like you."

Ellen said, "It's what Jesus would do, okay?"

Aunt Agatha said, "Plenty of white trash around here need saving."

Ellen said, "Please, can everyone be quiet? I'm listening."

Odysseus proclaimed, "But the Anti-Saloon League's goal is to ban intoxicants in Texas and in the whole U.S.A."

Many in the crowd said, "Amen."

Dad asked, "And what about the people who don't *want* beer and wine banned?"

Ellen giggled. "People such as Johnny?"

Richard gave Ellen a look.

Aunt Agatha said to Dad, "Your friend the darky is a Sabbath-breaker and a drunk. Most Mondays, Franklin is late with my ice."

Odysseus proclaimed, "Good Christians, help us free our nation from the liquor interests."

Dad said, "Watch out, he'll ask for money."

Odysseus asked, "Will you come sign these pledge cards, that you will abstain from beer, wine, and spirits?"

Aunt Agatha grinned. "You were wrong, John."

Odysseus asked, "Will you help with money? The liquor interests lobby Congress, and it costs us to remind Washington what small-town Christian values are."

Dad smiled at Aunt Agatha.

Odysseus said, "Our enemies wrongly call us `Drys.' But we aren't against water, we're against poison. If you're against poison, please come forward now."

Ellen stood up to join the cause.

Dad said, "Ellie, I don't think marching for Prohibition is what Jesus would do."

Ellen, now unsure, went over to Brother Bob (who was at the serving table, putting seconds on his plate).

Ellen asked, "Would Jesus join the Anti-Saloon League?"

Brother Bob said, "Certainly."

"Why?"

Brother Bob said, "Jesus said, `Suffer the little children to come unto Me.' But a drunkard's children face starvation, neglect, and temptations to sin."

Ellen said, "Good enough reason."

She turned and walked toward Odysseus. After several seconds, Richard stood and also went toward Odysseus.

Chapter 3
Medicine Show

Seventeen days later (April 4th)

It was late afternoon as Richard drove a horse-drawn wagon over a dirt road, among the gentle hills of Central Texas. Bluebonnets were blooming.

Sitting beside Richard were Ellen and Lucretia, who was another young prohibitionist. In the bed of the wagon were three suitcases (two feminine, one masculine). The wagon approached the small town of McTavish, Texas.

The Tatevillers didn't react when they passed a series of three signs. The signs were set at the road's edge, each many feet from the next (like those for Burma Shave); but *these* signs laid out a Bible verse:

Abstain from fleshly lusts
Which war against the soul.
1 Pet. 2:11

Lucretia asked, "So what would Jesus do?"

Ellen said, "It boils down to: Love God, love your fellow man, and forgive your fellow man."

Lucretia said, "And how are you coming?"

Ellen said, "One man I find it hard to forgive."

Richard looked puzzled by Ellen's remark.

Lucretia said, "My church says if you don't forgive, you go to Hell when you die."

Ellen said, "Baptists don't believe that."

Lucretia asked, "What if you're wrong?"

****

One minute later

Lucretia pointed. "Look, a traveling show."

On the edge of town, just off the road, was a gaily-painted wagon. It had drawn a crowd.

Richard said, "Can't stop, Miss Phillips. McTavish has only one hotel, and horses can't see after dark."

Ellen pointed. "Richard, we *have to* stop. That's *Johnny's* show!"

"If the hotel fills up, we sleep in the wagon."

Ellen said, "Have I ever asked for anything before?"

Richard said, as he turned off the road, "Half an hour."

Ellen squeezed his hand hard.

Ellen said, "Oh Lucretia, I'm so excited! I've never seen my cousin's show."

****

When Johnny's wagon got closer, Ellen saw that it read at the top "Dr. X. Xerxes Olsen's Medicinal Elixir." In front of the wagon was a small stage; over the stage was an awning.

Standing on the stage were three people. The first was a small man in a big suit; clearly he was Timmy the comic. The second was a haughty beauty with a trained singing voice; she must be Carla. And then there was Johnny—charming, confident, and one of the five most beautiful men in the state of Texas (or so Ellen believed).

As Richard's wagon approached, and then Richard helped Ellen and Lucretia dismount, Johnny was addressing the audience—

"Good folks of McTavish, Doctor Olsen's Elixir is unequaled for all manner of ailments: children's cough or fever, `female complaints'—"

Timmy said, "Yeah? *I* got female complaints."

Johnny played along: "You do?"

Timmy said, "I got complaints about females every dang day." He jerked a thumb at Carla. "Starting with her."

Ellen, Lucretia, and the crowd laughed. Richard pulled out his pocket watch.

Richard said, "He's lying to those farmers."

Ellen replied, "He's *entertaining* those farmers."

Lucretia said, "Who cares? Just let me look at him."

Johnny said, "Doctor Olsen's Elixir is world-renowned for giving vigor to husbands, as Timmy and Carla will demonstrate. . . ."

From the wagon Carla got a fan, opening it and fanning herself as she moved to the front center of the stage.

Timmy threw his arms around her and puckered his lips as if kissing her. Carla yawned.

Then with her free hand, Carla pushed Timmy away. He fell on his rear. The crowd laughed.

Timmy got up and came to her again, arms out and lips puckered.

Carla shut the fan and held it out at chest level, stopping Timmy at a fan's-length away.

Timmy got an idea. He ran around behind Carla to sneak up on her from the other side.

Fan out at chest height again, Carla was one step ahead of Timmy.

In despair, Timmy slinked over to Johnny.

Meanwhile, Carla had turned her back on Timmy and yawned again as she idly fanned herself.

Johnny gave Timmy a bottle of Doctor Olsen's Elixir. Timmy took a swig.

Timmy looked amazed. He pointed to the bottle, then gave the townspeople a thumb-up.

Timmy did a happy-dance around the stage, repeatedly clicking his heels.

Carla turned to look at Timmy—first sidelong, then full-face in wonder.

As Carla rushed over to Timmy, he stopped dancing. He smiled knowingly. Her hands, meanwhile, were all over him. That is, she touched him everywhere above the waist.

Carla moved a few steps so that she was directly in front of Timmy, and her back to the audience. Carla kissed Timmy on the mouth.

Carla kicked one heel up, and fanned herself vigorously.

As Timmy and Carla bowed to the audience's applause—

Johnny said, "Doctor Olsen's Elixir is made with snake oil, from the fat of live rattlesnakes. At only three dollars for thirty-two ounces, that's less than ten cents an ounce."

****

Twenty minutes later

Johnny's cousin's beau had his pocket watch out, and the beau was pacing. A two-person carriage, which was the only other vehicle beside Richard's and Johnny's wagons, now was leaving.

Carla was putting unsold elixir back in the wagon as Timmy folded up the stage and Johnny was counting the money. Carla was singing "There's A Little Bit of Bad in Every Good Little Girl" as she worked.

Johnny said, "Forty-two dollars. So, Ellen, what brings you to this one-horse town?"

Timmy broke in: "*Seventeen* horses. I counted."

As Johnny stuffed the money in a pocket, his cousin gave him a hug. That hug lasted longer than was proper for a male cousin, Carla noticed.

Meanwhile, cousin Ellen was saying, "We're going to an Eighteenth Amendment rally in Waco tomorrow."

Johnny asked, "What's an Eighteenth Amendment?"

Ellen said, "You haven't heard? Richard's uncle is Senator Morris Sheppard, and today he turned in a law to outlaw demon rum."

Ellen's beau said, "Actually, it's not a law *yet*. That's why the Anti-Saloon League is holding rallies across America."

Carla stopped singing, then said, "Good, us normal people are safe. For now."

Carla give Ellen's beau a challenging look as she went back to singing.

Johnny said, "Ellie, Ellie. My own cousin, a crackpot?"

Then Johnny said to Lucretia, "Lovely lady, I guess you're a crackpot too? I'm sorry, I didn't get your name."

Carla was angry now. Johnny and she were almost married; how *dare* he flirt with that do-gooder!

Two can play that game, Carla thought.

Ellen turned to glance at Johnny for some reason. In that same moment, Carla gave Ellen's beau an *inviting* look. (He was a handsome man, so it wasn't really a hardship.) The man returned Carla's smoky look with a behind-closed-doors smile.

Ellen now turned to look at Carla, only to find that Carla was already looking directly at Ellen with a catty smile that said, *I've put one over on you.* Ellen looked puzzled.

Ellen said, "Lucretia, this is my cousin, Horace John `Johnny' Carter. Johnny, this is Miss Lucretia Ann Phillips."

Then Ellen, looking around, asked, "So where is Dr. X. Xerxes Olsen?"

Johnny said, "You're looking at him."

Ellen said, "Thought so. And what's in those bottles?"

Johnny said, "Snake oil, extracted by a secret Hopi Indian—"

Ellen, touching his arm, said, "Johnny."

Carla frowned.

Johnny lowered his voice and said, "Caramel, menthol, ground dried jalapeño peppers, and moonshine. *Lots* of moonshine."

Ellen's beau helped Timmy carry part of the stage to the wagon and load it. Carla smiled at the beau, who smiled back; twit Ellen missed it all.

Johnny picked up the last of the stage and loaded it into his wagon, then began to roll up the awning. Ellen watched him flex with a smile on her face, Carla noted.

****

Almost sunset

Ellen, her beau, and Lucretia were back in the beau's wagon. Johnny's wagon was itself ready to travel.

Ellen asked Timmy, "Do you know Jesus?"

Timmy cracked, "*Know* Him? He owes me twenty bucks."

The beau said, "Ellen, we're running late."

Ellen said, "We loved the show, didn't we, folks?"

Lucretia agreed wholeheartedly. The dour beau said nothing.

Johnny said, "Good, because this might be the last performance of the Doctor Olsen Players."

Lucretia asked, "*Why?*"

Carla said, "He has to play soldier."

Johnny said, "When we declare war on Germany, I'm joining the Army."

The beau said, "You're signing up as soon as the call goes out? You aren't smart, are you?"

Johnny said, "*Excuse* me?"

"First American soldiers to go over won't know squat. Fritz will grind you into sausage."

Johnny said, "Those sound like words of a coward."

"I'll wait for the draft. I'm no coward, but I'm no fool either."

Johnny said, "Come down here and call me a fool. Or stay there and I'll call you a coward."

The beau jumped down from the wagon to fight Johnny.

Ellen said, "Please *stop*, both of you."

Carla thought, *You don't know your cousin well, do you sweetie?*

****

In the time it took the man to jump down and put up his fists, Johnny knew all he needed to know about him. Starting with the fact that Richard's first move was to go to where, in order for Johnny to face him, Johnny had to turn his back on Ellen and Lucretia.

The fight lasted more than a minute, which was too bad for Ellen's beau. Johnny had been doing physical work every day, so he had speed and stamina; at one minute in, the city-slicker fella was wheezing, but Johnny wasn't.

Then the guy cheated, as Johnny had half-expected: Richard now threw dirt in Johnny's eyes.

With Johnny blinded for a second, Richard managed to score a fat lip on Johnny.

But even as Johnny was wiping the dirt from his eyes, he put a knee into Richard's stomach, then waited for Richard to stand.

Richard tried to put a knee into Johnny's groin, but Johnny swept Richard's legs out from under him.

Richard grabbed a handful of dirt as he stood, but the scheme didn't work a second time: Johnny's arm shot out just before Johnny was blinded.

Johnny knocked Richard out.

****

Three minutes later (sunset)

Ellen's beau's wagon left, with Ellen driving the horses and her beau semiconscious between Ellen and Lucretia.

Carla said to Timmy, "That's his cousin? She acts like his old sweetheart."

Ellen and Lucretia took no notice that they were passing a series of four roadside signs:

The heart is deceitful
Above all things
And desperately wicked.
Jer. 17:9

Chapter 4
Does Jabez Pay Too Much?

Eight months later (December 1917, at night)
In a Dallas liquor store

Mike Lovelace, owner of the liquor store, was giving Jabez and Joe a tour of his store by lantern light. The electricity was off, and there was two months' worth of dust on the goods. The men were dressed for temperatures near freezing.

Lovelace said, "Any time now, Dallas will repeal this idiot law." By which he meant *citywide Prohibition.*

Jabez said, "Yeah? So why you talking to me?"

Lovelace replied, "Damn thieves in Fort Worth won't offer shit for my inventory. Plus, they don't want the building."

Jabez said, "Same here. What do I want with a liquor store that can't sell liquor? It's been two months, and the Dry Law looks here to stay."

Jabez looked around, then said, "I figure the retail's worth ten thousand."

Lovelace said, "Twelve, and not a penny less."

Jabez answered, "Deal. I'll have it in cash, ten tomorrow morning."

Lovelace looked amazed, but managed to say, "And Merry Christmas to *you!*"

****

Five minutes later, Jabez was behind the wheel of his 1916 Model T, which was parked by the liquor store. Joe cranked the car to start it, then got in the passenger seat. Jabez drove away, careful of road ice.

Joe said, "Did you see that fella's face? I don't know nothing about liquor stores, but you paid too much."

Jabez said, "Ha. It's a steal."

"How you figure?"

Jabez said, "Right now, Dallas is Dry, and Fort Worth is Wet. But I think the do-gooders soon will make all of Texas Dry. Then where will Dallas folk go?"

Joe said, "Shreveport?"

Jabez said, "Too damned far. When Texas goes Dry, whatever bottles I got will be liquid gold."

Joe asked, "But what if the whole U.S. goes Dry?"

Jabez said, "Even sweeter, you watch."

Chapter 5
Letter To Richard

Five months later (April 1918)
Ellen's bedroom

Ellen, dressed in a nightgown, was about to write a letter by electric light. Stacked on the desk were copies of a religious tract, "Jesus and the Doughboy."

Ellen began her letter: "April 4, 1918. Dear Richard, I again pray that this letter finds you enjoying life, health, and intact limbs."

****

Ellen then wrote, "In Austin last Saturday, Lucretia and I attended a rally held because the Eighteenth Amendment is sure to be ratified. This rally was as blessed by Jesus as our Waco rally of a year ago."

As Ellen wrote, she remembered—

Earnest, well-dressed white people were holding a rally. Signs read:

"Dry Good—Wet Bad"
"Prohibit Poison"
"Save Our Children"
"Booze Destroys Families"
" 'Drink Beer!' Says Germany"
"For God and Home and USA"
"The Saloon Must Go"
etc.

Ellen and Lucretia sang, clapped, yelled, and waved their signs.

****

Ellen now wrote, "It's bedtime. Win the war and come home to me, dear Richard. How I yearn to be held in your arms. Love, Ellen."

Ellen picked up one of the "Jesus And The Doughboy" tracts, flipped through it, put it back, and went back to writing her letter.

Ellen wrote, "P.S. I am sending salvation tracts with this letter. I know you will do right with them, because you are such a strong Christian."

****

Three weeks later, when Ellen's letter arrived
A cafe in Paris, France

A hand turned over an empty wine bottle; two other bottles had already died. The hand belonged to Richard.

Richard and two other doughboy privates were at a table with three young French women. Richard's companion raised her eyebrow and stood. After checking his wallet, Richard tried to stand, but made a poor job of it.

Chapter 6
Firing Franklin

Four months later (August 1, 1918)

Ellen, with purse on her shoulder, stood outside the back door of Aunt Agatha's and Uncle Horace's house.

Aunt Agatha rushed to the back door and yanked it open. "Whew, you came just in time!"

Ellen stepped into the kitchen and asked, "For what?"

"The colored boy's next door!"

"Franklin's been bringing ice here for years. Why am I here?"

"Because I can't get Horace or your father to come home. They think Franklin won't dare try anything."

While Ellen puzzled over Aunt Agatha's remark, there was a knock at the back door. It was Franklin, who waited for Aunt Agatha to open the door.

When Franklin walked in, he carried a block of ice. "Good morning Miz Carter, Miss Frost."

While Franklin loaded the ice in the icebox—

Aunt Agatha said quietly to Ellen, "Did you smell him? He's been drinking."

Ellen murmured, "How? We have state Prohibition."

Aunt Agatha gave Ellen an exasperated look. By now Franklin was headed for the back door.

Aunt Agatha whispered, "If he touches me, run out that door screaming."

Aunt Agatha then said to Franklin, "*Ahem.* Tomorrow we're getting an electric refrigerator. We won't need you anymore."

Ellen saw Aunt Agatha tense, but Franklin only sighed.

"Yes'm," Franklin said. "But I be still owe for today."

"What, you think I'm trash? I'll pay you two dimes, and you can keep the change."

Franklin said, "You gots to use me a month to get the 16.7 cent a day. One day ice be fifty cent."

Aunt Agatha said, "*Fifty cents?* You uppity thieving jigaboo, get out!"

Franklin opened his tongs and headed for the icebox. "I going, but I taking my ice with me."

Aunt Agatha said, "Stay away from my icebox, boy, if you know what's good."

Ellen opened her purse. "Hold on, I have a fifty-cent piece."

Ellen found it, and held it out to Franklin.

Ellen explained to Aunt Agatha, "Scripture says, `Thou shalt not muzzle the ox that treadeth out the corn.' "

Aunt Agatha looked like she wanted to scream at Franklin and Ellen both.

As Franklin took Ellen's coin, he said, "Is I supposed to thank you?"

Ellen frowned. Behind her, the Tempter's voice purred, "What an ingrate, that nigger drunk! He should bow and scrape in front of you—after all, you saved him from maybe a lynching."

Chapter 7
Two Men In El Paso

Five months later (January 11, 1919)
Two months after Armistice
Near the Hotel Del Sol
El Paso, Texas

Richard climbed out of a taxi. On Richard's Army uniform was one medal, one war-service chevron, a discharge chevron, and a PFC's rank.

Richard was approached by a Mexican woman who was wearing a checkerboard blouse and a dark-red, ankle-length skirt. She had three children gathered around.

The woman begged, in a thick accent, "Please, money for my family?"

Richard ignored her and walked on.

Richard was now approached by a newsboy, who held up an *El Paso Times* newspaper. Before the boy could speak, Richard waved him away.

Richard walked away from the newsboy and up to a local man who sat in front of the Hotel Del Sol.

Richard asked, "Sir, do you know of a good clothing store around here?"

The man pointed to a sign. " 'William Wilson and Sons, Clothiers.' Best in El Paso."

Now Richard was approached by a Mexican boy. The boy recited (again, with an accent), "Mr. Soldier, Ciudad Juárez has many pretty girls. The prettiest are at El Cabaret Azteco."

Richard said, "Tell me more."

The local man said, "Ciudad Juárez also has pickpockets, con artists, and workout men. It's heaven to American criminals."

The shill-boy said, "Tourists are safe at El Cabaret Azteco."

Richard asked, "Why do American criminals come to Juárez?"

The local man said, "The banks. Stash your cash in Juárez, and the Bureau of Internal Revenue never knows it's there."

"Amazing," Richard said.

Richard said to the shill-boy, "Sorry, kid, next time."

The boy left. Richard headed for the tailor.

****

One minute later
Near The Hotel Del Sol

Johnny got out of an Army car. He waved to the driver (who waved back), then Johnny limped toward the entrance to the hotel.

Johnny's uniform had two medals, three war-service chevrons, a discharge chevron, and sergeant rank. Johnny didn't bend his right leg—it seemed the leg was splinted—yet his uniform had no wound chevron.

He was approached by a Mexican woman who wore a checkerboard blouse and an ankle-length skirt. Three children clung to that skirt.

The Mexican mother said in English, "Please, money for my family?"

Johnny opened up his wallet and gives her two dollars, a good amount of money in 1919. He said, "*Te ves honesto. ¿Por qué te ruego?*" You look honest. Why do you beg?

She replied, "*Nuestra casa fue destruida en la revolución.*" Our house was destroyed in the revolution.

Johnny said in Spanish, "It is always bad when children suffer. And your man?"

She answered, "Killed."

Johnny said, "I am looking for a brave Mexican man. I would pay you to introduce us."

"Why do you need this man?"

"Liquor smuggling."

She said in Spanish, "Perhaps I know someone."

Johnny said in Spanish, "I will talk to you tomorrow."

He waved to the woman's children as he walked away. He limped straight for the newsboy.

Johnny asked, "Hey kid, how's the Dry Amendment doing?"

The newsboy said, "Sir? I figured you'd want to read about our fighting the Bolshies. Or about Teddy's funeral."

"Later. Spill, kid, how's the Eighteenth Amendment?"

The newsboy said, "Twenty-two states, as of two days ago. The *Times* isn't interested in that."

The newsboy held up the January 11, 1919 *El Paso Times*. Nowhere was the Eighteenth Amendment mentioned on the front page.

Johnny said, "I know some prohibitionists. The *Times* better put on a helmet."

Johnny pulled out his pocket change and gave the newsboy a nickel.

The newsboy, while holding out the newspaper, said, "Here you—"

"Keep it. Nickel's a gift."

The newsboy said, "*Sir?*"

Johnny said, "Kid, I'm out of the Army, I'm alive, and trench foot is getting off easy."

Johnny shook the newsboy's hand and hobbled away. Johnny heard the newsboy ask the world, "So what happened to his leg?"

Johnny limped to the hotel, but he was accosted by a Mexican boy just outside the hotel. A local man watched.

The boy recited in English, "Mr. Soldier, Ciudad Juárez has many pretty girls. The prettiest are at El Cabaret Azteco."

Johnny said, "*Hombrito, dime: ¿Son las niñas del Cabaret Azteco tan bonita como sus hermanas?*" Little man, tell me: Are the girls at El Cabaret Azteco as pretty as your sisters?

The boy puffed out his chest and declared, "*Señor, sólo la Virgen María es más bonita que mis hermanas.*" Sir, only the Virgin Mary is prettier than my sisters.

Johnny said in Spanish, "I'm sure. And does your father go to El Cabaret Azteco?"

The boy paused, then said, "No, sir."

"Why not?"

"It is dangerous."

In Spanish, Johnny said to the boy, "You are honest. Your father and sisters must be proud of you."

In English, Johnny asked, "How do I get there?"

The local man said, "Soldier, that joint's full of men with nasty knives."

Johnny smiled. "That a fact?"

Johnny, with the Mexican boy's help, removed his right canvas legging. Johnny hiked up his pant leg and pulled out of his boot his "splint": the German S98/05 "butcher's bayonet," whose blade was just short of fifteen inches long.

Johnny smiled big. "Meet Fritz."

The Mexican boy and the local man looked amazed.

Chapter 8
She Could Be In Movies

Three months later (April 1919)
A bridal boutique in Waco, Texas

Ellen was counting money, in order to hand it to the salesclerk, as Mommy and Aunt Agatha watched.

Ellen said, "You know what? This is the perfect time to marry."

Mommy asked, "How so, honey?"

Ellen handed the clerk the money; the clerk counted it.

Ellen said, "All my children will be born into a Dry paradise: safe roads, safe factories, honest elections, and where children get enough to eat."

The salesclerk said, "It's a lovely gown you selected. We can do your next fitting in two weeks."

Ellen said, "That long?"

The woman shrugged. "April is a busy time, dear. And Waco has many more June weddings than a small town."

****

One minute later
Outside in Waco's shopping district

Ellen, Mommy, and Aunt Agatha all carried shopping bags as they walked.

The three women passed an empty storefront. On the glass of the storefront were pasted many handbills. Each handbill read, "Let not your heart be troubled, neither let it be afraid. John 14:27"

The women's walking took them in front of a portrait studio.

Ellen said, "Maybe I'd better make an appointment if I want an engagement photo."

****

In the portrait studio, the display room was in front; the posing studio and the darkroom presumably were in back, past a doorway that was filled with a black slit curtain.

When Ellen, Mommy, and Aunt Agatha had opened the front door, a buzzer had sounded. Now the photographer came out through the curtain.

The photographer said, "May I help—oh my."

Mommy asked, "Something wrong?"

The photographer said to Ellen, "Miss, are you here to have your portrait taken?"

Ellen said, "I'm here to make an appointment for an engagement set."

"Are you free now? You're pretty enough to be in the flicks, and I want to take a set of you."

Hearing the words *pretty enough to be in the flicks* made Ellen feel raw panic. Ellen wanted to flee this man before he captured her like an animal.

Ellen said, "No."

Mommy said, "We don't want to buy two sets of pictures."

The photographer said, "No charge. Her portrait will be great for business. Really, she could be in movies."

Ellen choked.

Aunt Agatha said, "A *free* portrait? Ellen, don't stand there, go with him."

Ellen repeated, more forcefully, "*No.*"

The photographer said, "Yes, Miss Ellen, if you'll just step though the black curtain—"

Ellen yelled, "*NO!*"

Mommy and Aunt Agatha both looked confused and distressed. Because no way could they guess what was wrong with Ellen.

Mommy asked, "Ellen? What's wrong?"

Ellen said, "He can't make me go back there. No way, never again."

The photographer now was looking at Ellen the way that people look at dangerous lunatics. Meanwhile, Mommy's eyes were searching Ellen's face.

The photographer said, "Um, sure. Listen, I have prints to put in water bath. I guess I don't have time, after—"

Aunt Agatha asked, "What about the engagement set? Can we make an appointment for—"

The photographer said, "*No!* That is, unless one of you is with her at all times."

Ellen nodded emphatically. "Please, don't leave me alone with him."

****

Ellen jerked open the door and fled outside. Mommy and Aunt Agatha followed—Aunt Agatha looked puzzled; Mommy, worried. Ellen felt as if she'd escaped a dragon.

Ellen stopped in front of the empty storefront. Now its handbills read, "Forgive, and ye shall be forgiven. Luke 6:37"

Mommy asked, "What went on in there?"

Ellen's answer was no answer: "Hot for April, isn't it?"

Chapter 9
Wedding Night

Two months later (June 1919)
In a honeymoon suite

On Ellen's and Richard's wedding night, it was storming outside. A different kind of storm was raging inside.

Richard said, "You've misled me."

Ellen couldn't tell Richard the truth. Instead, she said, "No, I haven't misled you. I haven't."

Richard said, "So much goddamn work to get you here, then you aren't *intact*."

Ellen lied: "I'm still—I was fourteen, riding a horse."

Richard sneered, "Was the `horse' named *Johnny?*"

Ellen didn't say *No*. Instead, she asked, "Have I ever acted loose?"

Richard said, "Hell, right now you're a goddamn cold fish. How can you be frigid and a slut both?"

Ellen held out her arms. "I will make it good for you, my husband. Just be patient."

Richard said, "Ellen, while I was trying to start you, were you wishing I was Johnny?"

Ellen said, "Johnny is my cousin."

After a pause, Richard moved back into Ellen's embrace.

****

Thirty minutes later

Ellen and Richard were having sex, as the thunderstorm continued.

Ellen said, "Oh Richard, Richard, oh yes."

Ellen was close.

Ellen said, "Oh, *yes*. Oh, *yes*."

Just before Ellen climaxed, lightning flashed. And as she climaxed—

Ellen cried out, "*Johnny!*"

But a thunder boom drowned out her voice.

Richard could not hear what Ellen yelled, and Ellen did not realize her mistake.

Chapter 10
An Uncle In High Places

One month later (July 1919)
In the living room of Ellen's and Richard's house

The phone technician was demonstrating the use of a wall-mounted telephone to Ellen and Richard. Then the newlyweds walked him to the front door.

At the door, the phone technician said, "If you decide to upgrade from a party line, telephone our business office."

After the phone technician left, Richard took a paper from his pocket and went to the phone.

Ellen asked, "Who's that?"

Richard said, "Uncle Morris. I've decided to be a prohibition agent."

"But the Prohibition Unit wants law-enforcement experience. You'll never get the job."

Richard said, "They aren't under Civil Service. With a senator's referral, I'm in."

"So you call the Tateville operator, Tateville calls Waco, Waco calls Austin, then Austin calls Washington. We can't afford to feed and clothe so many operators."

Ellen could be so slow sometimes. Richard said, "A telegram can get lost."

Ellen said, "Then let's pray. I have a bad feeling about this."

They went to their knees and closed their eyes. After a ten-count, Richard opened his eyes and stood. "Jesus says he's okay with it."

As he went to the phone, Ellen also jumped up. She said, "My bad feeling, I think it's from the Lord."

I get so sick of her holier-than-thou dance sometimes, Richard thought.

He picked up the phone, listened, then hung up. He said to Ellen, "Mrs. Wagner's talking to some man. Ellie, you say Jesus wants Prohibition. So I'll be doing what Jesus wants."

Ellen said, "Mr. Barker pays you a decent wage. You don't need this."

Again Richard picked up the phone, listened briefly, then hung up.

Richard said, "Ellie, the Germans tried to kill me for a full year. I know how to take care of myself."

Again Richard picked up the phone and listened. He glanced at his paper as Ellen tugged at his arm.

Ellen said, "Please don't—"

Richard heard, "Operator. What number do you wish to call?"

Richard said, "Hello, operator? I'd like Washington, D.C., number Main-3120, branch 174."

As Richard went back to listening and waiting—

Ellen said, "Don't. You'll probably be fired soon."

"Why will I get fired?"

Ellen said, "Americans obey the law. When the government realizes this, most prohibition agents will be sacked."

Richard said, "And maybe I'll be lucky—hello, I'm Richard Sheppard, and I wish to speak to Uncle Morris."

*I'M GOIN' TO SETTLE DOWN, OUTSIDE OF
LONDON TOWN,*
Down in a village by the sea,
And you will find me there, with the country air,
Where everything is free.
*And when I'm over there, my heart will still be
here,*
And I hate to say goodbye,
But I'm a man who must have a little liquor
When I'm dry, dry, dry.

*—I'M GOIN' TO SETTLE DOWN, OUTSIDE OF
LONDON TOWN (1919) (McCarthy/Monaco)*

Prohibition that's the name
Prohibition drives me insane
I'm so thirsty, soon I'll die
I'm simply goin' to 'vaporate, I'm just that dry

I wouldn't mind to live forever in a trench
Just if my daily thirst they only let me quench
And not with Bevo or Ginger Ale
I want the real stuff by the pail

I've got the blues, I've got the blues
I've got the ALCOHOLIC BLUES
No more beer, my heart to cheer
Goodbye whiskey, you used to make me frisky
So long highball, so long gin
Oh, tell me when you comin' back agin

—ALCOHOLIC BLUES (1919) (Laska/von Tilzer)

VERSE 1: Down in my cellar, down in my cellar,
I've been changing ev'rything around.
I've a secret hidden there, I'll guard it with my life.

There's only one mistake I made: I told it to my wife.

CHORUS: Now EV'RYBODY WANTS A KEY TO MY CELLAR,
My cellar, my cellar,
People who before wouldn't give me a tumble,
Even perfect strangers are beginning to grumble,
'Cause I won't let them have a key to my cellar,
They'll never get in, just let them try.
They can have my money, they can have my car,
They can have my wife, if they want to go that far,
But they can't have the key that opens my cellar,
If the whole darn world goes dry.

VERSE 2: Now, down in my cellar, down in my cellar,
I've been having parties ev'ry night.
People that I never knew come up and talk to me.
They're trying hard to find out where I hang my cellar key.

—EVERYBODY WANTS A KEY TO MY CELLAR
(1919) (Rose, Baskette, Pollack)

Verse 1: The first of July [1919] they said we'd go dry,
And ev'ry one thought there'd be nothing to buy.
But you got yours, and I got mine,
And ev'ry one was happy we were feeling fine.
But soon we'll be through, then won't we feel blue,
No more we'll hear that "have another" sound.
Can you picture me saying "gimme some tea"
When Mister January [1920] comes around?

Chorus 1: WHOA JANUARY, oh January,
I hate to see you come 'round

July was mighty tough, but we could get enough,
And if we knew the barman we could get the
reg'lar stuff.
But oh January, WHOA JANUARY,
I'm so sad I want to cry.
You're the month that's going to make my life a
wreck;
I know I will turn into a horse's neck!
WHOA JANUARY, when you go dry
You're going to be worse than July.

Verse 2: Last night in a dream, how real it did
seem,
A raspberry soda all smothered with cream,
Said peek-a-boo I'll get you soon,
The time is coming when you have to use a spoon!
They filled you I hear with two percent beer,
But soon you'll be an ice-cream soda hound.
There's drinks we can pick, but not one with a kick,
When Mister January comes around.

Chorus 2: WHOA JANUARY, oh January,
I hate to see you come 'round
July you made us think we couldn't get a drink,
But when we wanted something all we had to do
was wink.
But oh January, WHOA JANUARY,
Sop long good old rock and rye.
Mister Bevo never made a hit with me.
'Cause it hasn't got the right authority.
WHOA JANUARY, when you go dry
You're going to be worse than Ju-, going to be
worse than Ju-, Going to be worse than July.

—WHOA JANUARY (YOU'RE GOING TO BE
WORSE THAN JULY) (Sterling/von Tilzer)

Chapter 11
One Day Before
(Constitutional)
Prohibition

Six months later: January 15, 1920
Lawn around the Copperas County courthouse
Tateville, Texas

Richard shouted to Lucretia, "The Prohibition Bureau office is in Dallas, but I'll travel all over Texas." He showed Lucretia his Prohibition Agent badge.

There was a Prohibition rally in progress, which made things noisy enough that Richard had to shout to be heard. But the noise level could be worse: A brass band waited nearby, but was not yet playing.

Ellen had worked for Prohibition for almost three years, but now that it was only one day away, she felt misgivings.

And not only because of Richard working for the Prohibition Bureau. But in that way, Ellen was very alone: Every "Dry" at the rally except Ellen was joyous.

Watching everyone at the rally was Sheriff Don, a likable man. At the moment, old Mrs. Carter and the Widow Manx were speaking with him, as Sheriff Don acted important.

At the edge of the crowd, farmers and ranchers listened, unimpressed. Ellen saw Johnny talking to some of them during the rally.

Off by themselves, several colored men and women watched the rally. They were miserable as they heard the bombast of the rally's current speaker, Elimelech Marshall.

Marshall was saying, ". . .Now for an era of clear thinking and clean living. Everyone, shake hands with Uncle Sam and board his water wagon."

The crowd cheered and applauded. Johnny continued to glad-hand farmers and ranchers at the edge of the crowd.

Marshall proclaimed, "They are dead, that sought the child's life. King Alcohol has slain more children than Herod ever did. As we grow better and stronger through the good influence of Prohibition, we will be in a position to give greater aid to the world."

Again the crowd cheered and applauded. Johnny now talked to rugged Amos. Each man, Johnny and Amos, eyed Richard.

Marshall proclaimed, "The reign of tears is over. The slums will soon be only a memory. We will turn our prisons into factories; our jails, into storehouses. Men will walk upright now, women will smile, and children will laugh. Hell will be forever for rent."

Now Amos left Johnny and walked toward Richard, as the brass band started playing and people started singing.

(Meanwhile, one colored man spoke to another, then their unhappy group left.)

****

A farmer whom Richard had noticed talking with Johnny, now walked over to Richard. "Mr. Sheppard? I understand you're a prohibition agent."

Richard glanced at Ellen. Good, Ellen didn't look suspicious. Richard led the farmer out beyond the throng.

The farmer said to Richard, "I'm Amos Walker, and my farm is on County Road 24. Listen, if you hear talk I'm cooking a still, it ain't true."

Amos pulled out a fifty and handed it to Richard. Richard was both insulted and tempted.

Richard said, "What's this?"

Amos said, "More than a week's pay for you. And all you have to do is save yourself a tour of County Road 24."

Richard shoved the bill back into Amos's pocket—but didn't let go of the money. Richard pulled his hand back, but couldn't make himself stick the bill in his own pocket.

Several times Richard moved the bill closer to either Amos or to himself, before finally shoving the money into his pocket.

Richard said, "But only for you. And you still better worry about Sheriff Don."

****

The two earnest old ladies who had talking to Sheriff Don had by then been replaced by Johnny. Ellen saw Johnny slap Sheriff Don on the back.

Seconds later, Richard rejoined Ellen at the rally. He looked happy.

Ellen asked, "What did Mr. Walker want?"

"He asked about hard cider. I told him it's allowed."

Ellen accepted that, trusting Richard.

Chapter 12
Blind Pigs And Clean Sheets

Three months later (April 1920)
Frost's Hardware And Lumber, Tateville

Ellen's father John, behind the counter, was handing change to Farmer Wilson, who had a coil of copper tubing over one shoulder. Ellen stood near her father; she'd been visiting him at the store.

Ellen asked, "Mr. Wilson, may I ask what you plan with that copper tubing?"

Farmer Wilson said, "Refrigeration. I'm building a coldroom."

Dad's face didn't show Ellen whether he believed his customer or not. Farmer Wilson tipped his hat to Ellen and left.

Ellen remarked, "Suddenly everyone wants copper tubing."

Dad said, "It's not illegal for me to sell. The last three months haven't changed that."

Ellen was puzzled. "What does Prohibition have to do with copper tubing?"

Dad was saved from answering when another customer approached the register.

Ellen said, "Time to go cook supper. Bye, Dad."

Ellen walked to the front door. But she was stopped by the young hardware clerk, Larry. Near him stood a travelling salesman, whose manner at first seemed furtive.

Larry told the travelling salesman, "This is the owner's daughter. She maybe can tell you."

Larry said to Ellen, "He's looking for a `blind pig,' he says."

Ellen said, "Try the livestock auction? But I'm sure all the hogs have eyesight."

The salesman said, "You don't get around much, do you?"

As Ellen acted puzzled, Dad walked up. With a gesture, Dad dismissed Larry. Dad said, "May I help you, sir?"

The salesman said, "I'm looking for a `blind pig.' "

Dad said, "Try the feed store, other side of the square. They might know."

The salesman said, "Much obliged."

Then the salesman asked, his manner no longer furtive, "Say, can you recommend a good hotel?"

Before Dad could answer, Ellen did: "The Bluebonnet Hotel, three blocks east. Clean sheets, fair prices, and most rooms have ceiling fans."

The travelling salesman made his goodbyes and left.

Dad said, "Ellie, a `blind pig' is a disguised saloon."

Ellen couldn't believe it: "Mr. Harper is breaking Prohibition laws?"

Dad asked, "Why didn't you mention the Tateville Hotel?"

Dad's manner was casual, but his question made Ellen tense. She replied, "Mr. Nelson once did me a favor, so I throw business to the Bluebonnet."

"Oh? What favor?"

Ellen said, "Richard's supper will be late. Later, Dad."

Ellen pecked Dad on the cheek and rushed out the front door, before Dad could ask her anything more.

Chapter 13
Richard Upholds (Some Of) The Law

The next morning
Downtown Dallas

Richard was dressed like a laborer.

He walked around a street corner. At the corner was Black Bull Saloon, which looked boarded up. Richard continued around the corner to the next business, Gonzalez Laundry, which was open. Richard walked in.

****

The laundry clerk looked up from his book as Richard entered. In the back, two women quit loafing and went to work doing laundry.

The laundry clerk said, "May I help you, sir?"

Richard said, "Bubba sent me."

The laundry clerk said, "You go back, turn right."

Richard went into the back. The two women "laundry workers" quit pretending to work.

On the laundry's right wall, five feet from the back wall, was a new door. At eye height was a peep slide.

Richard went to the door and knocked. The slide opened, showing a man's suspicious eyes.

****

The man outside the door said, "Bubba sent me."

Jabez asked, "What's Bubba's last name?"

The man rolled his eyes. "How the hell would *I* know? He's in Receiving, I'm in Shipping."

Jabez still felt suspicion, enough so that he didn't react for several seconds. Then at last Jabez slid the bolt and opened the door.

****

The man behind the peep slide opened the door to let Richard enter. Each man looked the other over. Richard tried to look harmless.

There were a dozen male customers in the Black Bull Saloon. At the barstool-less bar, a college-age couple was drinking and flirting. As Richard found his own place at the bar, he was surprised to see the girl there. But the bartender took no notice of her.

Richard said to the bartender, "Never been in a blind pig before. What you got?"

The bartender said, "Needle beer, wine, home brew, shine, rum, and Canadian."

Richard asked, "What's `needle beer'?"

"Near-beer with alcohol added."

Richard said, "Sounds good."

"Pay up first. Quarter."

As Richard put a quarter on the bar, he remarked, "Wasn't too long ago, beer was a nickel, and women never came in these places."

The bartender said, "Get used to it—"

The bartender took the quarter, then drew a half-percent-alcohol beer. He produced a syringe and injected a measured amount (marked with a pen on the outside of the syringe) of clear liquid into the beer. The bartender pushed the beer toward Richard.

The bartender finished talking: "—times have changed."

Richard took a small sip of beer. Then he said, "They sure have."

Richard pulled out his badge. "Prohibition Agent! You're under arrest."

From Richard's left pocket he pulled out a pistol, which he aimed at the bartender. Meanwhile, from Richard's right pocket he exchanged the badge for a small clean bottle and a cap. He dumped beer into the bottle and capped it one-handed, then put the bottle into his pocket.

****

The bartender put his hands up. Meanwhile, the customers fled through the door; Jabez had to jump back out of the way. Only then could Jabez draw his gun. But as soon as Jabez had a clear shot, the prohibition agent already had his own gun aimed.

The prohibition agent said, "Stop. I was gonna just arrest your bartender, but you twitch and I'll shoot you down."

Jabez said, "Yeah, you're `just' gonna arrest Henry— then tomorrow you Feds will be back with a court order and a padlock."

The "laborer" smiled. "That's the berries, all right."

Jabez said, "There's another way to go. Henry, put the cashbox on the counter."

Henry did so.

Jabez said, "I'll give you fifty to forget this, and two-fifty a week to keep it forgot."

The prohibition agent said, "One hundred and five hundred, or I march Henry out of here."

Jabez said, "One hundred now, two-fifty weekly."

"Hello, Mr. Padlock."

Jabez said, "If I give the word, *you'll* be the man shot down. Big D has lots of unemployed veterans."

****

Richard said, "Put the two-fifty with the hundred right now, I walk. But give me a boo-hoo how you're short, Henry walks with me."

At a nod from the saloon owner, the bartender put down his hands. The saloon owner went to the cashbox as Richard pocketed his gun. Seconds later, Richard was pocketing cash.

****

Meanwhile, elsewhere in downtown Dallas
In a former Army-uniform factory, now speakeasy

Johnny was speaking with the speakeasy owner, Charlie, while Johnny sniffed an open liquor bottle.

Johnny said, "Jeez, how much you paying for this panther sweat?"

Charlie answered, "Sixty bucks a case."

Johnny capped the bottle and put it down. "From me, fifty bucks."

"*Yeah?*"

Johnny said, "And if you want rye, scotch, or tequila, or good beer and wine, I can get you those. Real Kentucky bourbon, not moonshine with a fake label."

"No shit?"

Then Charlie got second thoughts for some reason. "I'd better not."

"*Why?*"

Charlie said, "The fellow who sells to me, I don't think he'd like it if I quit."

Johnny shrugged. "So his feelings get hurt."

Charlie said, "But he scares me. He *really* scares me."

Chapter 14
Touring Johnny's Farm

The next day
Jabez's brothel, room 15

Jabez and Joe were talking. Annabelle cowered in a corner. Which was about as far as the chain that was attached to the collar around Annabelle's neck, would let her get from the bed.

Jabez now said, "I am *very* pissed. I've lost two customers just yesterday."

Joe asked, "Boss, is it smart to be yapping so open-like?" He jerked a thumb toward Annabelle.

Jabez said, "Haw, you worried she gonna drag that bed to a police station?"

"Guess not."

"Anyway, I don't even know who's hitting me. Have you heard about anyone starting up as a boot?"

Joe said, "Nobody new."

Jabez said, "Find out who's hurting me. I want his name, where his base is, how many boys he's got. The little shit hurts *me*, I want to hurt *him*."

****

Meanwhile, in Frost's Hardware And Lumber, Tateville

At the front door, Larry pointed Ellen back to the office. In the store office, Ellen found her father with Johnny.

Ellen threw her arms around Johnny in a fierce hug. The hug ran several seconds longer than women usually hugged their cousins for.

Ellen said, "You rascal. Where have you been?"

Johnny said, "El Paso, Fort Worth, Dallas, Austin, and . . . my farm."

"*Farm?*"

Dad said, "He bought Hiram Pidcoke's 142 acres."

Johnny said, "Thank God for cash and the recession."

Ellen asked, "Where did you get cash enough for a 142-acre farm?"

Johnny looked amused for some reason. "Oh, Ellie."

Dad said, "The same place he got cash for lots of copper tubing and lumber."

Ellen said, "You're a *bootlegger?*"

Dad said, "Honey, it's time to grow up."

Johnny said, "Want to see my setup?"

Ellen said, "But Brother Bob—"

"If all you do is *look*, he'll let you back in the Baptist church. Probably. Maybe. I think."

****

Ten minutes later
In Johnny's car

Johnny, with Ellen his passenger, was driving on a dirt farm road. Ellen was very aware of Johnny's good looks.

Without reacting, the cousins passed a series of four roadside signs:

> *Flee also youthful lusts:*
> *But follow righteousness,*
> *Faith, charity, peace.*
> *2 Tim. 2:22*

Ellen asked, "Why are you breaking the law like this? Bootlegging is *illegal.*"

One of Johnny's strong hands on the steering wheel made a gesture. Johnny answered, "Money. You can't believe the money I make."

"But liquor and breaking the law both are unchristian."

Johnny's strong shoulders shrugged. Johnny said, "This law is silly."

"God hates drunkenness, so Prohibition is a Christian law."

Johnny's mouth laughed. Then Johnny said, "Oh, Ellie."

"There are pirates and hijackers out there. You could be killed."

Johnny stopped the car. Johnny's eyes turned to look at Ellen. "If you play safe in life, then you're already dead."

****

Five minutes later
The car arrives at Johnny's farm

The barn doors were open; Ellen saw trucks being loaded. In the hayloft a man with a rifle watched. Johnny's car drove up and parked; Ellen and Johnny got out.

Near the farmhouse was an underground tornado shelter.

Ellen's reaction to everything she was seeing? She gasped. "My word."

And what was it that she was seeing? The barn was packed solid with jugs of moonshine, cases of every kind of liquor and wine, and kegs of beer.

Johnny said, "C'mon, I'll show you my still."

****

Five minutes later

The still, which was far from the barn in a field, was huge (several hundred gallons' capacity). It was in use as the cousins drove up.

The still's odor made Ellen queasy. The closer she got, the more nauseous she got.

Johnny got out of the car and walked toward the still, clearly proud of it. Ellen reluctantly followed him.

Johnny said, "Sure, I buy hooch from neighbors, but *real* profit comes when I make it myself."

Johnny inhaled deeply. "Bet you've never smelled anything like this before, huh Ellie?"

Ellen vomited in the dirt.

Chapter 15
He Gets A Phone Call

That night
At Ellen's and Richard's house

The dining-room table was set for dinner. Richard and Ellen sat saying grace.

Richard and Ellen said together, "Amen."

Richard raised his head quicker than did Ellen. As Richard reached for food—

Ellen said, "Dear, I have special news for you."

Before Ellen could say more, the telephone rang.

Richard went into the living room to answer it. He said into the mouthpiece, "Richard Sheppard here."

The caller had an old woman's voice: "That no-account Johnny Carter bought Pidcoke's farm. He's bootlegging there."

Richard looked over to Ellen, his suspicions renewed.

Richard said, "He bought a farm? Thanks for the tip, ma'am."

Richard hung up the phone, then stomped back to the dining-room table to take his seat.

Ellen said, "Congratulations, you're going to be a father."

Richard said, "Did you know your cousin Johnny just bought a farm?"

"Honey, did you hear me? I'm expecting."

"He grew up in town, but he bought a farm. Did you know that?"

Ellen said, "Please, this should be a joyous moment."

Richard repeated the question: "Did you know Johnny bought a farm?"

"Yes, he showed me this morning."

"What did you see there?"

"A-a farmhouse. He has a cute little farmhouse."

Richard said, "Caller says Johnny's using the farm to bootleg."

Ellen said, "You're angry at me. Let's pray over this."

" `Pray'? You're a fine one."

Ellen felt hurt. Changing the subject, Ellen said, "If it's a girl, I want to name her Carol."

"Why not Joannie or Joanne? Janet? Why not name her after her father?"

Ellen glared. "That was unchristian."

****

The next day
In the Dallas office of the Prohibition Bureau

In the office was an outer office of fourteen desks, and a glassed-in inner office. Of the fourteen desks, two desks had secretaries, seven desks were vacant, two desks were vacant and also bare, and two desks had men writing reports.

At the fourteenth desk, a prohibition agent, Eb, was talking on a desktop telephone.

In the glassed-in inner office, behind the desk sat Richard's boss Mike; Richard stood in front of him. Richard was excited; Mike was playing sourpuss.

Mike said, "One old granny on the telephone? That's what you got?"

Richard said, "But I *know* the bum. He's as wet as the Red River, I'm sure."

Mike said, "And I'm sure that Johnny Carter of Tateville is a simple cotton farmer. Request for raid denied."

Richard said, "Give me two men—"

Mike said, "Denied. One other agent: denied."

Richard said, "That's a swell Cadillac sedan you bought last week, *sir*. Did your wife ask how you could afford it?"

****

That afternoon
In a federal judge's chambers

Richard was in front of a federal judge, who was reviewing Richard's search warrant.

The judge said, "Twice you've misspelled *alcohol*."

Richard couldn't figure this guy. "But you'll sign?"

The judge said, "A woman stranger telephoned and said this man's a bootlegger, no evidence offered. This is your `probable cause'?"

"I figure she's a law-abiding citizen."

The judge said, "Bookkeepers figure, policemen find out the facts."

The judge shoved the warrant at Richard. "This is amateur. Denied."

PART 2
Prohibition In
Practice, 1924

Chapter 16
Look What I Found!

Almost five years later (December 1924)
Johnny's farm and farmhouse

Prohibition had been good to Johnny. The barn of 1920 had been enlarged so that it more resembled a warehouse; and a watchtower had been built high up, by the fence. Up in that watchtower, Chris the rifle-toting tower guard watched the dirt road with binoculars; a closed-circuit phone was within reach.

Near the warehouse was a water tank for fires. Also near the warehouse, five moonshine stills were in use.

At the edge of the property, men with Thompson submachine guns patrolled on horseback.

The grass was brown, with no snow. The temperature was in the thirties, which was typical of a December day.

By the farmhouse was parked a car marked "Copperas County Sheriff." Sheriff Don came out, sticking a thick white envelope into his overcoat. Sheriff Don got into his car and drove back to town over the dirt farm road.

Approaching the farm from town was a car. Chris checked out the car through binoculars, then made a phone call:

"Johnny? Ellen's coming."

****

Ellen, nine months pregnant, walked into the kitchen of the farmhouse as Johnny was talking to three other men. With Ellen was cute Carol, age 4, whom Johnny doted on.

Little Carol carried a chocolate cake on a cake tray, as serious as though she held the British Crown Jewels.

Johnny smiled. "Carol cutie, did you bake us a cake?"

Carol stood straight. "Mommy made it. But I helped a lot."

Ellen put the cake tray on the table. From her coat pocket, Ellen took religious tracts, which she also put on the table. Ellen unbuttoned Carol's coat, then her own.

Carol pulled out a rag doll from her coat pocket, sat on the floor, and began playing.

Ellen asked, "Did I pass Sheriff Don on my way here?"

Johnny said, "Yep."

Ellen sighed. "Sheriff Don too?"

Johnny grinned. "Sheriff Don too."

"But Richard's still straight up."

****

Meanwhile, in El Banco Comercial de Matamoros

Richard was at a teller window with a shoebox, the lid of which he opened. Inside were cash bills.

Richard dumped the money on the counter. The Mexican teller counted the money twice.

"Three thousand, two hundred and sixty-four dollars," the teller announced.

Richard smiled. "That's right." He lay a Banco Comercial passbook on the counter. "Put it all in here."

****

In Johnny's kitchen, Carol saw something interesting under the table. She crawled under to investigate.

Johnny said to Ellen, "Richard hasn't taken *my* money. Myself, I think it's only because I cleaned his clock seven years ago."

Ellen said, "That's not true. I know Richard is honest."

From under the table, Carol called out, "Mommy, look what I found."

Carol crawled out from under the table, holding Johnny's bayonet.

Horrified Ellen snatched it away.

Amused Johnny took the bayonet from Ellen and—while pointing the bayonet at the ceiling—wagged a finger at Carol.

Johnny said to Ellen, "But I'll tell you, I know of *one* honest flatfoot out there."

Ellen said, "Oh? Who?"

Johnny said, "Whoever tossed Woody into the Waco clink."

****

One hour later
Tateville Barber Shop

Ellen and Mommy stood just inside the door. The shop had two barber chairs, each with customer and barber—Dad was one of the customers.

A man waiting, Jake, drank home-brew from a blue glass bottle. Ellen frowned, seeing that.

Mommy said, "John, talk to your daughter. Visiting the Waco jail, my word!"

Dad said, "Ellen Mary Frost Sheppard, you know better."

Ellen said, "God commanded it, so God will protect me."

Dad's barber said, "Churches got programs to visit prisoners, Mrs. Sheppard."

Ellen said, "Will Woody listen to someone he's never met?"

Dad's barber said, "You shouldn't be around Johnny's gang. Some rough characters there."

Ellen gestured toward Jake. "Wonderful. You men buy hooch from Johnny's gang, but you don't want me to show them Christ's love."

Jake said, "I didn't get this from Johnny. I bought it from—"

Dad said, "Someone Richard might arrest."

Jake said, "—from someone here."

Ellen frowned at Dad. "Aren't you my father?"

Chapter 17
Visiting Woody In Jail

Two hours later
Waco jail, Visitor's Room

Bars separated visitors and visited.

A jail guard who held a clipboard didn't look impressed with Ellen. Nervous Ellen carried her purse and a Bible.

The jail guard demanded, "Your name, and prisoner's name?"

Ellen said, "Ellen Frost Sheppard, here to see Woody Mahler."

The jail guard wrote down this information, then said, "Lemme see those."

Ellen handed over her purse and Bible. The jail guard went through them with suspicious thoroughness, then handed them back.

The jail guard said, "Take a seat."

As Ellen took the one vacant visitor's chair, the jail guard handed the clipboard to one of two guards on the prisoner side.

The prisoner-side guard disappeared with the clipboard through a door in the back. In the second that the door was open, many male voices yelling could be heard.

Another prisoner already in the room spoke louder than before—

"Goddamn it, I'm innocent, I hardly touched her!"

The disappeared guard opened the door, escorting Woody, who turned out to be a man in his forties whom Ellen had seen around Johnny's farm a few times.

While the door was open, again many male voices yelling could be heard, including a voice saying—

"—your rotten hands off me!"

Woody sat in the only vacant prisoner's chair, as Ellen now wished she were anywhere else. But Ellen had a job to do.

Woody said, "The Prohibition Unit got women doing its work now?"

Ellen said, "I do not my husband's work, but the work of my Father in heaven."

"It's you Bible-thumpers who put me in jail in the first place."

Ellen felt dismayed by Woody's attitude. Aloud she said, "Jesus will give you peace during this troubling time."

Woody said, "`How do you feel, Woody? Is there anything you need, Woody?' Yes ma'am, I need some smokes and a lawyer."

Ellen said, "I care about you as a person, not a do-gooder project. How do I convince you?"

Woody said, "Lady, I'm in serious shit: I was caught hauling hooch. Want me to trust you? Tell me serious shit from your own life."

Ellen said, "There is no `serious stuff' in my life."

Woody said, "This from the woman hot to get poked by her own cousin."

Ellen said, "I want no such thing!"

Woody stood. "Guard? I'm ready to go back now."

Ellen said, "Wait, I'll tell you something I could never tell my folks."

Woody sat.

Ellen said, "May 1916, a stranger came into Dad's hardware store. His name was Danny Payne, and oh, was he dressed sharp!"

Woody asked, "Traveling salesman?"

Ellen said, "Said he was a movie scout."

"Bet he told you, `You'll be a silent-screen star.' "

Ellen sighed. "That's why I went to the Bluebonnet Hotel for a script reading."

The jail guard said, "Time! Visitors, step away from the prisoners."

All visitors but Ellen stood.

Ellen said, "But I'm not done with my story."

The jail guard said, "Ma'am, step away from him *now*."

As Ellen stood up, she said to Woody, "I want to visit you tomorrow."

Woody said, "I ain't sure—you haven't told me nothing."

****

One hour later
On the dirt road between Waco and Tateville

Ellen, alone in her car, was talking to God.

Ellen prayed, "Lord Jesus, you told us to forgive those who wrong us, and to pray for them. You know why it is so hard for me to forgive Mr. Danny Payne. I pray for strength to someday forgive him. Amen."

Ellen's car passed a series of four roadside signs:

If ye forgive men
Your Heavenly Father
Will also forgive you.
Matt. 6:14

Chapter 18
Two Fake Script
Readings

That night
Jabez's brothel, Room 15

Annabelle lay dead on the bed, strangled by her own chain. Joe and Steve were holding a struggling naked man, while Jabez examined Annabelle's injuries.

Jabez said to the naked man, "Mister, if you didn't like the sex, you should've talked to me."

Jabez said to Joe, "Leave Annabelle's body one place, his another. Then tomorrow we find us another whore."

****

The next day

Jabez's car was stopped on a dirt road by a sign: "Graves, Texas—Small Means We're Friendly."

Joe was swapping a California license plate for the original Texas license plate, as Jabez waited behind the wheel.

****

Fifteen minutes later
In the one ice cream parlor in Graves, Texas

By the window, a young beauty was reading a movie magazine and eating vanilla ice cream, as Jabez walked in the front door. She was stylishly, but not provocatively, dressed.

The same could be said for Jabez: now he was dressed well—a regular Joe Brooks—but he was clearly no pantywaist.

While Jabez waited for his ice-cream order, he looked the girl over. When she noticed him noticing her, she gave him a shy smile and returned to her reading.

When Jabez got his ice cream, he took a table next to the young beauty.

Jabez asked, "Enjoying your magazine?"

The girl said, "I love reading about photo-play actresses."

"Then this might be your lucky day. Maybe. I don't want to get your hopes up."

"Hopes up about what?"

Jabez handed her a business card, and smiled. "You're pretty enough for a movie."

The girl read the card: "'Daniel Payne, Casting Scout.'"

She looked puzzled.

Jabez said, "Cecil B. DeMille plans to shoot a western near here. My job is to find him a lead actress. May I know your name?"

The girl said, "Gracious. But why not the Gish sisters? Or Norma Talmadge? Oh gracious, I'm Millicent Laird. But call me Millie." Millie put out her hand.

Jabez shook Millie's hand as he laughed. "Because those big actresses now demand *ten thousand* a *week*. You'll be as pretty, but cheaper."

Millie thought about that.

Jabez's expression didn't change, but he worried: *Will she realize this sounds too good to be true?*

But then Millie nodded, accepting the explanation.

Jabez said, "Have you ever performed at anything, Millie? Ever done mime?"

"I've studied dance, a little. Probably not enough? Maybe I should forget this. But. . ."

Jabez said, "Yes?"

"What would I get paid? *If.*"

"Three-fifty a week."

"*Three hundred fi*—! Oh, mercy." Millie smiled, lost in fantasy.

Jabez said, "But I don't want to get your hopes up, even though your look is perfect."

Jabez wondered: *Is Millie hooked? Will she go along with what I say now?*

Millie leaned forward, her eyes glittering. "Goodness gracious. What do you need me to do?"

"I'm staying in Room Eight at the hotel. When would be a good time tonight for you to read?"

Millie asked, "Is eight okay?"

"Eight's fine."

"Gracious, Mom and Dad will be *thrilled.*"

"*No!* Look, the reading might not go well, or Mr. DeMille might not like you. Save yourself embarrassment till your chances look good."

Millie thought about that.

Jabez wondered: *Does she see the danger? Will she tell me to scram?*

Then Millie grinned. "Room Eight, at eight, *secret* meeting. Deal."

****

That night
Jabez's hotel room in Graves, Texas

The room included a window, a bed, one chair, and a closet. The closet door was shut. A movie script lay on the chair.

Someone knocked on the door. Jabez went to the door and opened it. Millie stood just outside.

****

Woody said, "Okay, so then you went to his room. Then what?"

Jabez invited Millie in, and gestured her to the chair while he sat on a corner of the bed. His manner was businesslike.

Ellen said, "He invited me in. He didn't act like a parlor-snake, he was very serious."

Millie picked up the movie script as if it were a holy relic, then sat down.

Ellen said, "The movie script was waiting on a chair. It was like Christmas morning when I got the script in my hands."

Jabez and Millie made small talk. She kept handling the script.

Ellen said, "Mr. Payne talked with me, trying to relax me. But I so wanted to start my reading."

Jabez pointed to the script, and Millie found the page. Millie and Jabez both moved to the window and started hammy acting.

Ellen said, "Finally, he gave me a scene to read."

Woody asked, "Remember what it was?"

Ellen said, "He was a mean banker, and I was asking him to give my father a few more days. Mr. Payne performed without a script."

Jabez stopped Millie, and directed her to a new place in the script. They moved together in what would have been a romantic scene, except that Millie had to constantly refer to the script.

Ellen said, "Then we did a scene where I pretended I was in love with the mean banker. He touched me, he kissed me, and he got fresh, while I acted drunk with love."

Jabez stopped Millie, and directed her to a third place in the script. She moved to the window, standing with her back to Jabez. Jabez went to the far side of the bed and went down on his knees.

Ellen said, "Then I read my `goodbye' speech. I was to say it with my back to the mean banker."

As Millie performed, Jabez pulled out a brown glass bottle from under the bed, and opened its cap. From his pocket he took a handkerchief.

Ellen said, "It was long and corny. `Clarence, I said you were the stars in my sky. . .'"

Jabez poured liquid from the bottle onto the handkerchief, then quickly put the cap back on. Jabez crept up on Millie. Who still was reading from the script, and still had her back to Jabez.

Ellen said, "`. . .I said you were the rose in my garden, I said your voice was to me like the song of birds.' And then. . ."

Jabez now was behind Millie. He shot his hand forward to press the handkerchief over Millie's nose and mouth, while his other arm snaked around Millie's waist. It took only seconds for her to slump.

Ellen said, "Suddenly he covered my nose with a smelly cloth. Chloroform. I don't remember anything after that."

****

Jabez's hotel room in Graves, Texas

Unconscious Millie had been tossed on the bed. Jabez opened the closet door; Joe stepped out.

Jabez said, "Now the fun begins."

The men began yanking and ripping Millie's clothes off.

Joe asked, "Did you chloroform her enough?"

Jabez said, "I learn from experience, got it? She'll sleep till Calvin Coolidge has kittens."

Jabez got naked enough for sex, and mounted passed-out Millie. The sex was hard, brutal.

Jabez remarked, "It's so exciting when they're helpless. Besides, it makes them so much easier to manage afterward."

Joe said, "Boss? I think she moved."

Jabez, while still using Millie, replied, "If she wakes up, give her another whiff of chloroform. You bet, I learn from experience."

****

May, 1916
Room 8, Bluebonnet Hotel, Tateville

Ellen said, "When I woke up—Woody, this was horrible."

Danny Payne, naked, was using naked Ellen. Her eyes fluttered open.

Woozy Ellen said, "Hurts."

"Son of a bitch!" Danny Payne exclaimed.

Payne slugged Ellen hard.

Ellen asked, "What you doing?"

Payne said, "I'm enjoying you, stupid cunt."

He slugged Ellen again; she whimpered. She tried to push him off; she couldn't. Her hand flailing around found the bottle on the nightstand. She grabbed the bottle.

Ellen tried to hit Danny Payne in the face with the bottle. She missed, but Payne got a whiff of chloroform fumes. For some seconds he was distracted, and Ellen tried to roll out from him.

But Payne recovered, and threw the bottle against the door. Glass shattered and liquid splattered everywhere.

He grabbed Ellen. "You're not getting away."

Through the door came the voice of John Nelson, who owned the Bluebonnet: "What's going on?"

Payne said, "A lover's spat."

Ellen managed to say, "Mr. Nelson? Help?"

Payne said, "*Shut up*, you."

Ellen screamed. Payne slugged Ellen and she stopped screaming, as footsteps behind the door ran away.

Footsteps ran up to the door, a shotgun was pumped, then the door flew open. Nelson held a shotgun level at Danny Payne.

Nelson said, "Get away from Miss Frost."

Payne said, "She wants it."

Nelson said, "Miss Frost? Is that—?"

In the second that Nelson looked at Ellen, naked Jabez lunged at him. He pushed the shotgun up out of the way, then flattened Nelson as he ran out the door.

Footsteps ran away, a door slammed, a Cadillac was self-started and then driven away.

****

December 1924
Waco Jail visitor's room

Ellen had been making a second visit to Woody.

Ellen said, "Mr. Nelson took me home. Dad was at the hardware store, and Mommy at sewing circle—they never knew my shame."

Woody asked, "What happened to Payne?"

Ellen said, "Back to California, I hope."

****

Three hours later
Jabez's brothel, Room 15

Millie, in lingerie, now was the woeful girl chained to the bed. She was held captive by Joe and Steve, as Jabez injected her with a syringe.

Chapter 19
Gotcha!

Meanwhile, in the Dallas office of the Prohibition Bureau

Richard walked in to the office to see, through the glass, Mike cleaning out his desk. Eb was just hanging up his telephone, so Richard went to Eb's desk.

At a different desk, a man whom Richard had never seen before, was discussing a report with a prohibition agent. The stranger was acting like the boss.

Richard asked, "Hey Eb, what's the story?"

Eb said, "Mike got caught taking scratch. Meet Vernon, the new boss."

"This is acey-deucey! I've got a plan now, and it's sweet."

Richard rushed over to Vernon. Seconds later, when Richard happened to glance in Eb's direction, Richard saw that Eb looked thoughtful.

****

One hour later
Judge's chamber

Richard was pushing a warrant before the same federal judge who had denied him a warrant before (April 1920).

The judge was suspicious. "This man, Moses McCoy, sells liquor to grade-schoolers?"

Richard said, "And often to high-schoolers."

The judge said, "Which is bad, but not so as bad as selling to small children."

Richard said, "Of course, you don't want to know what happened after that sixteen-year-old girl drank the moonshine."

"What happened?"

Richard said, "Your Honor, do you have a daughter? What's the worst you can imagine?"

The judge flipped to the last page, scribbled, then thrust the document out to Richard.

****

Courthouse lobby

Connie was a twenty-three-year-old flapper, currently sitting on an uncomfortable hardwood bench. She stood up as Richard walked up.

A clearly overjoyed Richard waved the signed search warrant around like it were a Fourth of July sparkler.

Connie said, "You look happy."

Richard said, "Yep. The search warrant is for a made-up bootlegger. The judge didn't notice I put Johnny's name on the signature page."

Connie hugged and kissed Richard. "Ain't you the cat's pajamas."

Richard said, "Oh *Johnny*, I have your ass now."

Connie smiled to herself. Now she wouldn't need to worry about rent on her apartment for at least a month.

Chapter 20
The Farm Gets Raided

The next day
Dallas office of the Prohibition Bureau

The outer-office desk count: two secretarial desks, three desks bare, and nine desks claimed. All nine prohibition agents were in the office: Fred, Zach, Ted, and four other agents waited to make a raid; Eb was on the phone; and Richard was in the inner office, talking to the boss.

Vernon said, "He tried to *bribe* you?"

Richard said, "I threw the money back at him. But I'm sure Johnny's slipped cash to at least one man here."

Vernon said, "Think so? Tateville's a long way from Dallas."

Richard said, "Sir, don't tell our boys anything till the end. Else Johnny will find out about this raid."

Vernon said, "*I'll* worry about what to say and when, got it?"

****

Meanwhile, at Johnny's farm

Johnny stood at one of his stills, talking to a distiller. Neither man seemed excited or worried.

****

One hour later
In front of a country store

Eight trucks and a car were gathered together just off the (paved) road, in front of a country store. Richard was driving the lone car, with Vernon climbing out of the passenger seat.

By the store was a telephone booth. By the road, a sign read "WACO 79."

Vernon yelled, *"Listen up, men, now I can tell you the plan. We are headed for the town of. . .?"*

Richard said, "Tateville."

"—of Tateville to raid a major bootlegger. His name is—"

Richard said, "—Sir, don't."

Vernon said, "Not now. *His name is John Carter.—*"

Eb said, "And Richard here wants his ass."

Vernon yelled, *"Today we will shut down his business and take away his freedom. Saddle up."*

Fred said, "I need to telephone my wife."

Vernon asked, "What for?"

"I'll be late for supper."

Vernon said, "Make it quick."

Fred headed for the phone booth. Alarmed, Richard jumped out of the car and dashed for the phone booth. Fred started to run too.

But Richard got to the phone booth first.

Richard said, "I just remembered, *I* have to telephone *my* wife."

Richard jerked the handset cable out of the box. He smirked as he said, "But the telephone is broke."

Fred said, "You pecker! No way can I live on forty bucks a week."

Vernon asked, "What are you two arguing about?"

****

Meanwhile, in front of Johnny's barn/warehouse

Johnny was talking to one of his truck drivers. Neither man seemed worried or excited.

****

Three hours later

On a paved highway, Vernon's convoy passed a sign, "WACO 7."

****

Meanwhile, on Johnny's farm

In a field, Johnny was talking with two workers. Those two men were doing something with shovels and a wheelbarrow that was filled with dirt. Everyone was calm and unworried.

****

One hour later

On a dirt road, the car and eight trucks passed a sign, "McTAVISH 12 TATEVILLE 31."

****

Meanwhile, in Johnny's kitchen

Johnny was talking with three men. Everyone was calm, unworried.

****

One hour later

On a dirt road, Vernon's convoy passed a sign, "TATEVILLE 6."

****

Meanwhile, on Johnny's farm

Johnny was up in the watchtower, talking with Chris the tower guard. Chris seemed bored and sleepy.

Johnny could understand why. Looking around from the watchtower, all Johnny could see were dirt roads and farmland. Nobody was farming their farmland in December, and nobody was driving on any of the dirt roads that Johnny could see.

****

Thirty minutes later
Entrance to Johnny's farm

The prohibition vehicles were parked just outside Johnny's property. The prohibition agents were being met by Johnny and his guards; Richard held out the search warrant. Nobody pointed his weapon, but many men (both prohibition agents and Johnny's men) held them.

Richard said, "Horace John Carter, we have a warrant to—"

Johnny said, "Cut the applesauce. Let's get this over with."

Johnny gestured to his men: "Stand down."

****

Johnny's barn/warehouse

The barn had its doors shut. Parked in front of the barn was a truck, its cab loaded with kegs. Leaning against the barn was an ax.

Richard ran to get the ax. Vernon directed the other agents: Eb, Zach, and Jim to check the barn; Ted, Matt, and Paul to check out the stills; and Fred and Bobby to investigate the farmhouse and tornado shelter.

By the time Richard stood by the kegs, holding the ax, Johnny was there too.

Richard said, "I'm about to cook your ass."

Johnny said, "So chop."

****

At the tornado shelter

The tornado shelter was a room-sized hole in the ground. Wooden steps led down from ground level. The floors, walls, and steps were covered with boards. The steps were sheltered by two heavy doors which laid almost horizontal, just inches above ground level.

Fred and Bobby opened the doors and stepped down into the shelter. The tornado shelter looked empty—just board surfaces, one table and two chairs, and a kerosene lantern. The men glanced at each other, climbed the stairs, and shut the doors.

****

Meanwhile, outside the barn

Richard hacked into a keg with Johnny's ax; beer poured out.

Richard grinned. "Johnny, you're under arrest—"

"Taste it," Johnny said.

Vernon tasted it. "No kick."

Johnny smiled at Richard. "Half-a-percent alcohol. Legal in all forty-eight states."

As Richard looked at the beer stream in shock—

Zach yelled, "Vernon, we got a problem."

Richard and Vernon looked in Zach's direction. The barn doors were open, and the barn was empty.

While Richard and Vernon were staring at the barn—

Ted yelled, "Shit. *Vernon!*"

****

By Johnny's stills

Richard and Vernon ran up to join Ted and the other two agents at the stills. Behind them, Johnny was strolling their way.

The stills not only were shut down, they were also punched through with dozens of ax-holes.

Richard said, "He couldn't move the stills, so he got rid of the moonshine."

Ted asked, "So why isn't the ground wet?"

Richard said, "He moved the dirt."

Vernon said, "He wins—search warrant won't let us check dirt."

Johnny had now joined the five prohibition agents. He said, "These were here when I bought the farm—I was shocked. First day, chopped 'em up."

Vernon eyed Johnny. "Yeah, I'm sure."

Vernon turned around to yell, "*Hey everyone, back to Dallas.*"

Richard begged, "Don't quit now."

Vernon said, "We won't find anything if we search till sunset."

Richard glared at Johnny. "I *will* come back."

****

Five minutes later
The entrance to Johnny's farm

The prohibition agents were about to enter their various trucks—except Richard, who rushed Eb.

Richard said, "You fink rat. You telephoned him!"

Richard threw a punch. Eb blocked it, then punched Richard in the stomach.

As Richard struggled to breathe—

Eb lowered his voice so Vernon couldn't hear: "My sheba-baby don't come cheap."

Chapter 21
But Would Jesus Do THAT?

Meanwhile, Waco Jail visitor's room

Ellen was visiting Woody a third time.

Now Woody was blushing. "I, um, have a favor to ask."

"Yes?"

Woody pulled a paper from his pocket. "It's my mother. I don't know how often you're in Dallas, but—could you see if she's okay?"

The Tempter said, <<You're a wife, you're a mother, you don't have time for this! He wants you to motor all the way to Dallas and visit a woman you've never met? Tell him no!>>

The gentle voice said, ++The job needs doing, and there is nobody else Woody can ask.++

Ellen decided, *I'll do it. Lord, I pray that You find a way that visiting Woody's mother will lead him to the Lord.*

The gentle voice's answer was puzzling: ++Your prayer is heard. Remember that all things work together for good for those who love God and are called according to his purpose.++

Ellen took the paper from Woody. "I'll go today, no problem."

****

Ten minutes later
In a Waco phone booth

In the background as Ellen talked were identical posters pasted to the side of a building:

*For I am come to set the daughter against her
mother. Matt. 10:35*

Mommy said over the phone, "I see a problem."

Ellen said, "I'm doing the Lord's work."

Mommy said, "Do you realize how late you'll come pick up Carol? Even later, if you nail a tube or boil your radiator over?"

"I'm driving to Dallas, not Detroit."

"Brother Bob tells me you're neglecting Carol and endangering your unborn."

"Tell Brother Bob I have faith in the Lord."

Mommy said, "Besides, Dallas has churches who can call on Mrs. Pruitt."

Ellen said, "`Let George do it' is not in my Bible."

"Here's a text that is: `Honor thy father and mother.' Once again I have to change my plans because of you."

****

Four hours later
Parlor of Mrs. Pruitt's house

Ellen was visiting with Mrs. Pruitt, who turned out to be a woman in her sixties, and who moved slowly.

In the parlor was a grandfather clock; the time was 5:04. (Meaning, roughly half an hour before sunset.)

At the moment, Ellen was laughing. "That Woody, how funny."

Mrs. Pruitt said, "Oh dear, the time. Child, I think you should say goodbye now."

Ellen was puzzled. "Have I offended you?"

"Dallas isn't safe for a woman after dark. Not since we went Dry."

"Oh? Dallas has so many churches."

"But Dallas also has speakeasies galore, and drunken automobile races, and fighting."

Ellen said, "I'm sure Houston and Austin are worse."

"I hear Dallas has a bordello where the girls are chained to beds."

Ellen shrugged. She saw no connection between that somewhere-in-Dallas bordello and her own life.

But then Ellen politely said, "How horrible."

The doorbell rang, alarming Mrs. Pruitt. "I'm not expecting anyone."

Ellen said, "Let *me* get the door."

Ten seconds later, surprised Ellen held the door open, as Johnny swept in carrying a box of groceries. Mrs. Pruitt watched from a safe distance.

Ellen asked, "What are you doing here?"

Johnny said, "The same as you, I reckon: looking out for Woody's mother."

****

Almost sunset
On the street in front of Mrs. Pruitt's house

Johnny and Ellen stood near their automobiles.

Ellen opened her purse, saying, "New tracts. Please read them."

She pulled out two religious tracts and gave them to Johnny. The two tracts were "Are you good enough for Heaven?" and "Drunkenness and God's Word."

Johnny said, "Did you know John Hancock smuggled liquor? Him and me, we're striking a blow for freedom."

Ellen said, "Oh you! In 1917, didn't you sell disguised liquor to suckers?"

That was a cheap shot, and Johnny frowned.

He asked, "Cousin, have you ever gotten drunk?"

"I took the pledge almost eight years ago. I've never tasted alcohol."

"So why the hell are you preaching about something you ain't never done?" Johnny let the *Drunkenness* tract drop to the street.

Ellen said, "I haven't jumped off a building either, but I can still warn you against it."

Ellen tapped the other tract, which Johnny still held. "And *you* are still a *sinner* and need Jesus."

"Stop, I've heard it. I'm the bad son, I need Jesus, I'll go to hell, so on, so on, so on."

Ellen asked, "Have you heard about Johnny Torrio?"

"He a Mexican?"

Ellen said, "He's a crook in Chicago, and he's killing other crooks over bootlegging. Listen, you can get killed."

Johnny said, "That does it! Tell me, would Jesus go into a speakeasy?"

"Yes, Jesus never let human rules stop Him from saving souls."

Johnny said, "Then brush your hair. I'm taking you to a speak near the Adolphus."

"You're taking *me* to a speakeasy?"

"Richard won't be home tonight, and Aunt Audrey already has Carol."

"But Brother Bob says—"

"Near the Adolphus Hotel downtown, I sell to a joint that hits on all six. That's where we'll go."

Ellen said, "I get it. You want to ruin me, so I can't witness to you anymore."

"*Wrong.* I've decided: Before you preach to me one more minute, you're gonna learn my world."

Ellen said, "You'd be shocked what I know about this nasty world."

"Such as, Some men spit on the sidewalk? Oh, the evil!"

Ellen had told Woody about her drugged rape by Danny Payne, saying it all without a qualm, because the Lord had directed her to speak out. But now, face-to-face with Johnny, Ellen couldn't whisper even one word of her sordid tale. As a result, Ellen couldn't argue Johnny's last remark.

Instead, Ellen said, "If this will make you listen when I share the gospel, I'll go."

Uneasy Ellen walked to the passenger door and got in Johnny's car.

Chapter 22
Ellen At The Speakeasy

Thirty minutes later
The Big D At Dark Club

A jazz band played as a woman sang, while two cigarette girls worked the room. Johnny and Ellen gave their hats and coats to a hat-check girl, then a hostess escorted the cousins to a table.

Many of the women customers were better dressed than Ellen. This made her even more self-conscious, beyond being nine months pregnant. Johnny also was underdressed, but seemed unbothered by it.

On the way to their table, Johnny and Ellen passed a swank teen couple. Several tables away, two young flappers kissed. Nobody (including Johnny) seemed bothered by the adolescents drinking or the young women kissing. Ellen didn't know what to think.

It was early in the evening; half the tables were empty.

Now seated, Johnny signaled to the sexier cigarette girl.

Ellen said, "Three tables over: They're children, and they're drinking."

Johnny said, "Oh dear, now this place will lose its saloon license."

The cigarette girl sashayed up. On her belt was a mechanical coin changer; the rest of her uniform was provocative.

The cigarette girl gave Johnny an inviting look that Ellen did not like *at all*. The cigarette girl gave Ellen a very brief look, but that look said *You're not in his league*. Ellen didn't like that second look either.

The cigarette girl said, "Good evening folks, I'm Susie. Can I interest the gentleman in cigars, and cigarettes for the lady?"

Susie's words mentioned Ellen, but Susie's body language ignored Ellen. Ellen felt annoyed.

Ellen said, "I don't smoke."

Susie gave Johnny a look that said *Poor man, what else does she not do?*

Susie said, "My mistake. You looked like you needed something *cylindrical*."

Johnny said, "A pack of Luckies, please."

Susie said, "Twenty-five cents, sir."

Johnny handed Susie a dollar; she handed back three quarters. In turn, Johnny tipped Susie two quarters. She handed Johnny a pack of Lucky Strikes, as—

Susie said, "The gentleman is *so* generous. Are you staying for the contest?"

Ellen's look asked, *What contest?* Johnny shrugged *No idea.*

Johnny said, "Probably not."

Susie said, "Pity. You'd do great."

Susie walked away, sashaying as she went. Johnny opened the pack and offered Ellen a cigarette. She declined.

Johnny casually remarked, "Gambling's in the other room. Want to try it?"

Ellen was horrified. Johnny lit a cigarette, grinning.

****

9:37 p.m.

The speakeasy's band was playing a fast song. The two lesbian flappers, along with many young normal couples, were dancing the Charleston.

The speakeasy was three-fourths full.

A group of speakeasy regulars was gathered around the cousins' table. Among them: a woman with a long string of pearls and a cigarette holder, a slick-haired man, and a man wearing a sack suit. Johnny said nothing to help Ellen as the drinkers gave her a hard time.

Johnny was drinking a beer; in front of Ellen was a bottle of Dr Pepper.

Ellen nodded toward the lesbian dancers (Lucy and Trudy). "Brother Bob would say those two are depraved, and that dance, indecent."

Slick-Haired Man said, "That? They look like chickens on a hot stove. Your preacher's a fool."

His scorn dismayed Ellen.

Long String Of Pearls said, "Next you Drys will outlaw radio, cigarettes, and Rudolph Valentino."

Ellen said, "But Demon Rum hurts your health, and makes families poor. We banned it for the greater good."

Sack Suit said, "Ma'am, I hate my boss. Either I drink, or I kill him."

"Have you tried talking to Jesus about your boss?"

Sack Suit paused to choose his words: "*Liquor*, I know, works."

The song and dance ended. Lucy and Trudy returned to their table only long enough to grab their drinks and join the throng by the cousins' table.

Lucy asked, "What are you talking about now?"

Long String Of Pearls said, "Mrs. Bluenose here wants to know why we drink giggle water instead of cold water."

Trudy said, "You're a *Dry?* You seem too nice."

Lucy said, "Since this is your first time, you *have to* stay for the contest!"

Ellen said, "What cont—?"

Susie walked up. "Cigars or cigarettes, anyone?"

None of the group was interested.

Susie looked straight into Johnny's eyes, struck a pose, and asked, "Sir, *anything* you need?"

Ellen did *not* like seeing Susie carry on like that.

Johnny said, "We're set, thanks."

Susie purred, "If you change your mind, tell me soon. I'm off at eleven."

Susie sashayed off, as Ellen stewed.

Slick-Haired Man said, "Folks, raise a glass to Prohibition: it made Fun against the law. And anything against the law is twice as fun."

Everyone but Ellen drank to that. Ellen was stunned that they couldn't see Prohibition's wisdom.

*****

10:57 p.m.

The room was packed. All the drinkers, including Lucy and Trudy, were back at their own tables. The band broke out into another fast song.

Lucy and Trudy stood up to dance, then called to Ellen.

Trudy said, "Want to learn the Charleston?"

Lucy said, "C'mon."

Ellen said, "You're kind to offer, but—"

Johnny said, "What, Jesus wouldn't Charleston?"

*****

10:59 p.m.

Lucy and Trudy danced the Charleston, while pregnant Ellen managed a toned-down copy.

Trudy said, "Must be confusing: Your preacher says don't drink, and Daddy there says it's okay."

Ellen said, "Johnny? He's my cousin, not my husband."

Lucy said, "*Whoops.* See, when the cigarette girl—your face—"

Ellen quickly changed the subject: "Why do y'all drink alcohol and come here?"

Lucy said, "Folks here are up front. Give them money, Trudy and I are welcome. But a church only treats you nice when you keep their rules."

Trudy said, "My reason for coming here is the contest. It's fixing to start."

Ellen asked, "*What* contest?"

A man in tails stepped up to a microphone and signaled the band to stop. In the sudden silence—

Trudy said, "The *kissing* contest!"

A technician pushed a rolling spotlight up next to the man in tails.

Man In Tails said, "Ladies and gentlemen, it's eleven p.m., time for our kissing contest. We'll let the dancers return to their seats."

As the three women returned to their seats, Ellen noted Susie selling tobacco to a couple. Susie looked impatient; Ellen remembered it was quitting time for the cigarette girl.

Man In Tails said, "Let's make this room romantic."

The lights dimmed except for the band, the bandleader, and the man in tails.

At the edge of the room, a door opened; a manager stepped into the room. He shut the door most of the way, but some light spilled through from the room beyond. Ellen could see the manager, side-lit. The manager looked at Susie.

Man In Tails held up cash. "I have fifty dollars for the best couple's kiss."

The crowd *ooh*ed and applauded.

Man In Tails said, "Any couple—man and woman, boy and girl, dog and cat."

Lucy and Trudy, and the teenage couple, yelled and clapped.

Man In Tails said, "Your applause will choose the winning couple. Who—"

Susie wiggled past the cousins' table on the way to her boss, giving Johnny a sexy smile. Ellen boiled.

Susie walked up to the manager. He followed her into the lit room beyond the door. The door shut; darkness returned.

"—wants to go first?" Man In Tails asked.

The spotlight moved over the crowd, finding couples who would stand and kiss. The teen couple and Lucy and Trudy were among many contestants. The audience approved of very passionate, theatrical, or funny kisses, while Man in Tails ad-libbed.

Man In Tails said, "Is that all? Ed, find us a couple who's got the goods."

In search of an attractive couple, the spotlight swept past Johnny and Ellen—

Man In Tails said, "Ed, back up. Stop, *them*."

The spotlight was on Johnny and Ellen.

Man In Tails said, "Kiss her good, sir, you win fifty clams. But remember: No whoopee!"

Johnny gestured *No*.

Man In Tails said, "Sir, you *know* how to kiss." He leered at Ellen's pregnancy. The crowd laughed.

****

As the crowd laughed, Johnny's nonverbal *No* got more forceful.

The manager's door opened, and Susie walked through. She'd swapped her coin changer and cigarette rack for a coat.

Man In Tails teased, "Sir, are you a he-man or an Ethel?"

Ellen saw Susie made a beeline for Johnny, as the crowd chanted, "*Kiss her! Kiss her!*"

Johnny said, "She's my cousin."

(But Johnny couldn't be heard over the crowd noise.)

Now Susie stood by Johnny.

Man In Tails said, "Look out, train wreck!"

Susie gave Ellen a contemptuous look and bent down to kiss Johnny. Normally a late-pregnancy woman isn't fast, but—

Ellen zoomed around the table—elbowing Susie aside—and grabbed Johnny's face. The kiss was scorching.

The crowd roared a cheer, and clapped.

Not soon enough, surprised Johnny pushed Ellen's face away from his own.

Johnny exclaimed, "What the hell!"

Ellen realized what she's done. She rushed from the room as—

Man In Tails asked, "Don't you want your fifty?"

****

The Dallas street outside the speakeasy

Ellen hurried out the boarded-up front door onto the sidewalk; Johnny rushed out after her. He felt disgusted, but he also felt confused: Why had Ellen done this?

Two other couples stood outside, flirting and smoking.

What the cousins had come out from seemed to be a boarded-up business, "Big D Removal and Freight Co." Pasted on the boarded-up windows were identical handbills:

*Then when lust hath conceived, it bringeth forth sin:
and sin, when it is finished, bringeth forth death.
Jas. 1:15*

Johnny heard, far in the distance, tires screeching as a car turned a corner at high speed.

Johnny said, "This was sick. You're sick."

Johnny heard the higher-pitched sounds of a car accelerating. The sounds were also getting louder.

Ellen said, "Johnny, please don't—I—"

From the sounds that the accelerating car was making, it was very close.

Johnny needed only a glance in the sounds' direction, then he wrapped arms around Ellen and pulled her down. *"Get down!"* he yelled.

Johnny covered Ellen's body with his own (as much as her huge belly allowed), but he was facing away from the street. He couldn't see whatever happened next.

One of the two other men dropped like Johnny. The third man, and both women, stood confused. The other dropper grabbed his date by the wrist and yanked her down.

****

Time crawled for Ellen.

Ellen saw a car race up, with the man of her nightmares hanging out the passenger-side window. Danny Payne held a Thompson submachine gun, which he fired as he got near.

Everything at waist level—the boarded windows, the handbills, the boarded-up door, and the two adults still standing—was hosed down. The car raced away.

The Bible-verse handbills had their text riddled with bullet holes. One handbill fluttered to the sidewalk.

****

The other surviving couple acted shocked by their close call as—

Johnny asked, "You okay? The baby okay?"

Johnny got up off of Ellen. He felt awkward around her, because of what had just happened inside.

Ellen said, "Johnny, I saw him."

"Who? That bastard Jabez?"

Ellen said, "Lord Jesus, strengthen me. It was Danny Payne!"

Johnny looked at her blankly. "*Who?*"

Chapter 23
No Such Fella

Forty minutes later
In the Dallas office of the Prohibition Bureau

Ellen and Richard were alone. Ellen was cleaning her scrapes with iodine. Richard was at a filing cabinet; he yanked out a file, skimmed it, then shoved it back in.

Richard asked, "Where's Johnny?"

Ellen said, "He knows better than to come here."

Richard said, "You're helping Johnny-boy instead of me. Surprise, surprise."

Richard slammed the drawer shut. "We have no record of any `Danny Payne' anywhere."

Ellen insisted, "It *was* Danny Payne."

Richard rushed over to Ellen, looming too close. "Where do you know him from? Danny Payne?"

Ellen said, "I can't tell you."

"What were you doing tonight with Johnny?"

Ellen said, "Winning him to Jesus, that's all." But she wouldn't look Richard in the eye.

Richard spotted the lie. He shook Ellen hard. "*What were you doing with Johnny?*"

"Hardly nothing."

Richard shoved Ellen to the floor. Iodine spilled.

Chapter 24
Betrayal

Fifteen minutes later
Jabez's warehouse

Dora and Francine were making fake whisky as Jabez checked their work.

Dora took fifth-bottles filled with a whisky-color liquid, capped each bottle, stuck a Jack Daniels label on the bottle, put a counterfeit Texas tax stamp on the bottle, and put the fake bottle on one of many shelves behind her.

Francine took, from a shelf behind her, a Mason jar filled with a colorless liquid. She unscrewed and discarded the lid. Using molasses and a glass stirring rod, she turned whisky-color the moonshine in the Mason jar. From a nearby crate of such bottles, she took several empty fifth-bottles; using a funnel, she filled the bottles from the Mason jar. When the Mason jar was empty, Warehouse Woman 2 got another from her shelves.

Jabez grabbed a fake Jack Daniels and shoved it under Dora's nose.

Jabez pointed. "Label's crooked."

It wasn't, and Jabez knew it wasn't. But Dora didn't defend herself, she cringed.

Dora said, "Sorry, I'll—"

A door slammed, a man's footsteps quickly approached, then Richard stormed up to Jabez and the women. The women continued working.

Richard said, "Jabez, need to talk."

Jabez said, "Why the hell are you here?"

"You want Johnny's secret base? I'll take you there, and to hell with whom I piss off."

Jabez asked, "So where is it, outside Fort Worth?"

Richard said, "Tateville."

Jabez murmured, "Where *you're* from."

Richard now was pacing, clearly upset. He said, "And Ellen's protecting the bastard. She admitted she went with him tonight to some speakeasy on Commerce, right?"

Jabez said, "On *Commerce?*"

"I ask questions, she invents booshwa how she's shot at by Danny Payne."

Jabez startled; Richard didn't seem to notice. Jabez now tried to pump Richard—

"A speakeasy on Commerce Street *was* hit tonight."

Richard said, "So what. Fed or flatfoot, nobody's heard of any `Danny Payne.' "

Richard doesn't suspect a thing! Jabez was relieved.

Then Francine spilled a teaspoon's worth of fake whisky. Angry Jabez rushed over to the frightened woman.

Jabez growled, "Your choice: the punch, or the dollar?"

Francine said, "I can't afford the dollar."

Jabez slugged Francine out of her chair. He said, "Do that again tonight, I'll dock you *and* hit you."

As frightened women go back to work, Jabez returned to Richard.

Jabez said, "You, me, and my boys will hit Johnny's place. If we suit up like prohibition agents, Johnny's gang will die before they suspect a thing."

Richard said, "Yeah, that's a smart plan."

Jabez slapped Richard on the back. "Which *you* made possible. Tell Lucas the cashier I give you two hours, and any of the thirty girls on the second floor."

Richard smiled. "Wow, thirty pieces of ass."

With a grin, Richard started for the door. But Jabez's gesture stopped him.

Jabez asked, "Does your wife Ellen like film plays?"

Puzzled Richard nodded.

Chapter 25
Brother Bob Visits Ellen

The next morning
Waco Jail visitor's room

Ellen had had three hours' sleep.

As a guard seated Woody, he said, "You look like shit. The flu?"

"Last night I went to a speakeasy with Johnny, and— Anyway, your trial's about to begin. Are—?"

Woody peered into her face. "Something happened last night."

Ellen took a long time to speak the words: "I kissed him."

Woody asked, "A *boy-girl* kiss?"

"I was so *proud* of myself. I felt so much holier than the others in church—"

Woody asked, "And holier than *me?*"

Ellen nodded. "And all the time I was both sinner and fool. Forgive me for how I've acted."

Woody said, "Let's pray that prayer now."

Ellen was beyond shock. "*Now* you'll accept Jesus?"

"From you, now I'll accept Jesus."

Woody bowed his head; Ellen followed.

Ellen recited (with Woody echoing), "Lord Jesus, I am a sinner, deserving eternal hell. . . ."

But this was no *rote* recitation for Ellen; she meant every word.

****

That afternoon
Living room of Ellen's/Richard's house

Carol played on the floor with her doll. Ellen opened the front door at the doorbell; Brother Bob entered.

Brother Bob said, "Hello Carol, that's a pretty doll. Sister Ellen—"

Carol said, "Would you like to have tea with us? Tracy came home—we're having a party."

Ellen said, "Carol, sweetie—"

Brother Bob said, "Your doll is gone a lot?"

Carol said, "Uh-huh. Tracy goes out to preach the Gospel to prisoners."

Brother Bob said, "And she's gone a lot."

As Carol nods—

Ellen said, "Sweetie, why don't you take your tea party to your room."

Carol and her doll left. Ellen hurried to change the subject: "So how are things with Julia?"

Brother Bob said, "Right now Julia is at Frost's Hardware, refrigerator shopping."

Ellen nodded. "Dad is selling them by the boxcar."

"Even more so, after what happened to Franklin."

Ellen said, "*Oh?* I haven't heard."

"Oh, that fool coon got himself half-blind from bad hooch."

When Ellen gave him a puzzled look, he explained, "He's lucky he didn't die. What he drank, it had wood alcohol mixed in with the grain alcohol. That's the risk those people take."

"That's *awful.*"

But Franklin was apparently not why Brother Bob came. He cleared his throat and said, "Sister Ellen, several folks at church are concerned about you and your children."

Ellen raised an eyebrow. "Really. And who are the people `concerned'?"

"Yesterday `the Lord's work' took you to Waco, then to Dallas. In Dallas you went to a speakeasy with your moonshiner cousin, and you were shot at."

"I was witnessing to him there."

Brother Bob said, "All this time Carol was without her mother."

Ellen said, "Yes, but the Apostle Peter left his wife at home to preach the gospel."

"And what about Carol, if her mother had been killed?"

Ellen said, "I am trusting the Lord God."

Brother Bob said, "You are *tempting* the Lord God. Your neglect endangers Carol's soul."

Ellen quoted Luke 9:59-60: "And Jesus said to another, Follow me. But he said, Lord, suffer me first to go and bury my father. Jesus said unto him, Let the dead bury their dead: but go thou and preach the kingdom of God."

"Jesus said this to a *he*, not a *she*. Paul wrote Titus that young Christian women should love their children, be keepers at home, and be obedient to their husbands."

Ellen said, "Reread Acts, chapter ten—when your interpretation of God's Book makes you disobey God's Word, your understanding is wrong."

Brother Bob was sarcastic: "I'm a preacher of the gospel, but I don't understand God's Word?"

Ellen didn't like Brother Bob's tone. She said, "Brother Bob, I'm missing time with my daughter to talk to you. So you'll be *pleased* when I throw you out."

Ellen went to the front door and jerked it open.

Going just outside the door, Brother Bob turned and faced Ellen. "Jesus said, `Forbid not little children to come unto me, for of such is the kingdom of God.' You will answer for the souls of Carol and your child to come."

Ellen counter-quoted, "Depart from me, into everlasting fire; I was a stranger, and ye took me not in; naked, and ye clothed me not; sick, and in prison, and ye visited me not."

****

Ellen shut the front door hard. She headed back to Carol's room.

During that walk, Ellen said (to a man who couldn't hear her), "Jesus calls on us to visit folks sick and in prison, Brother Bob. I won't ignore the Word of God."

Walking through the house, Ellen got a thought—which she hated.

Ellen shook her head. "Oh no. *No*, Lord Jesus, *please.*"

Ellen dropped to her knees, begging, "Don't send me *there!* Lord, I have to live in this town."

Ellen's talking brought Carol out of her room. Carol was holding her doll. "Who are you talking to, Mommy?"

Ellen said, "To God. Do you remember Franklin, who delivers ice?"

Carol nodded, looking puzzled.

Ellen said, "Franklin is sick. God wants me to visit him, but I don't want to go."

Carol asked, "Because he's colored?"

Ellen nodded.

Carol held out her doll. "Want to hold Tracy, mommy?"

"Why would I want to hold Tracy?"

Carol said, "Sometimes you tell me to do stuff I don't wanna do. Holding Tracy makes me feel better when I do it."

After a pause, Ellen took the doll.

Chapter 26
Johnny Babysits Carol

Early the next morning
In a Dallas garage

Richard, Joe, and hoodlums in cheap suits checked weapons. Sunlight shined through the windows at a low angle as Jabez rushed in.

Jabez asked, "Everybody ready?"

Joe said, "They're eager to go."

Jabez asked, "Fake warrant?"

Richard patted his coat pocket.

Jabez said, "*Mount up, fellas.* Let's go have fun at Johnny's farm."

****

Three hours later
Front yard of Ellen's/Richard's house

Johnny was at the street by his car, whose engine was running. Ellen started to walk Carol to Johnny's car.

Ellen said, "Johnny, I really appre—"

Johnny said, "*Stop.* I'll take Carol because Aunt Audrey's sick, but you stay back."

Johnny opened the passenger door for Carol.

Carol looked at her mother. "Is Uncle Johnny mad at you?"

Ellen said, "Cousin, I have greatly sinned."

Johnny nodded. "You have."

Johnny said to Carol, "Now, sugar cake, let's go have fun at my farm."

Carol got in the car, then Johnny got behind the wheel and drove away. During this, Johnny never looked at Ellen.

Chapter 27
Troubles For Ellen And Johnny

One hour later

Ellen's car was in the colored part of Tateville, and Ellen was drawing hostile stares. A baking dish with casserole was on the passenger seat of the car.

Ellen drove over dirt roads past a shabby church; its sign read "Jubilee African Methodist Church." A permanent part of that sign: "I can do all things through Christ which strengtheneth me. Phil. 4:13"

Ellen prayed, "Lord, what if I *don't want to* `do all things'? Please find someone else."

Ellen's car approached a cross in someone's front yard, with two colored men working around it. As Ellen got close, she saw that the cross has an odd, lumpy silhouette.

Up close, the cross was a smoking hulk. The men chopping down the cross glared at Ellen. She was stunned by what she saw.

Ellen prayed, "Lord, I'm not like the Klan. But these people frighten me! Let me obey you some other way."

But Ellen kept driving.

****

Five minutes later
In a grocery store in Colored Town

Ellen walked in the door. She saw only colored faces, none friendly. Ellen waddled up to the Counter Woman. From her frown, Counter Woman resented Ellen being there.

Ellen said, "Excuse me, I'm looking for Franklin the ice man."

Counter Woman asked, "What be his last name?"

Ellen said, "It's . . . I don't know."

"Figure." Then Counter Woman eyed Ellen's tummy. "What he done to you?"

"*This?* Don't be sil—not that he—I'm not after Franklin."

Counter Woman said, "You owes him money?"

"No. He's sick, and I want to visit him."

Counter Woman's face said, *I don't believe that.* What her mouth said was, "I don't know where he at."

Counter Woman turned away from Ellen, supposedly to wait on a customer. Nobody else spoke up, so Ellen left.

****

Ellen in Colored Town tried to find Franklin—

1) Ellen stood on a rickety porch, talking to two women in rockers. No luck.

2) Ellen stood by her idling car, talking to a man walking his dog. The man was stone-faced before he shrugged and went on.

3) Ellen stood outside the Jubilee Church, talking to a man who wore a suit with a cross lapel pin. His answer was no, and he acted skeptical of Ellen.

4) Ellen talked to five preschoolers. They were too young to know anything helpful, but they acted friendly. A girl felt Ellen's bulging abdomen.

5) Ellen talked to three teen boys. Nervous Ellen had one hand on the steering wheel and only one foot out of the car.

6) Ellen stood talking to two teenage girls holding a jump rope. Both girls pointed to Ellen's right.

****

Meanwhile, on Johnny's farm

Chris the tower guard was looking at Richard and the other Dallas people through his binoculars. But so far, he was holding only binoculars, not a gun.

Just beyond the farm entrance were the cars from Dallas. Richard stood holding up the search warrant. Jabez stayed in Richard's car, hat pulled low over his face. Two of Jabez's goons were smoking inside their respective cars.

****

Chris phoned Johnny.

Johnny said into the phone, "What's up, Chris?"

"Richard Sheppard is back, with another warrant."

Johnny said, "That's it! No more sugar to the Dallas office."

Chris said, "But I don't recognize these fellas. And Johnny?"

"Yeah?"

"One fella sitting in the front car won't let me look at him."

Johnny said over the phone, "*Yeah?* Let me look."

After a pause, Johnny cried, "It's Jabez—sound the alarm!"

Chapter 28
Ellen Visits Franklin

Franklin's front yard

As Ellen parked her car, she saw that Franklin was sitting in a rocker on his screened-in front porch. Near his rocker were two packing crates that were used as stools. Sitting on one of the crates was a colored girl in a faded red dress. The girl looked about ten years old.

The girl held a book in her hands, and was reading aloud to Franklin.

Ellen stepped out of her car (with her casserole dish) and walked toward the two coloreds on the porch.

As Ellen got close, she saw that the book that the girl was reading from, was *My Bondage And My Freedom* by Frederick Douglass.

". . . All was fair, thus far," the girl read, "and the contest was about equal. My resistance was entirely unexpected, and Covey was taken all aback by it . . ."

Then the girl noticed Ellen. She put the book down in her lap, saying to Franklin, "A white woman, she walking toward yo' house! And she expecting."

Franklin called out, "*Who there, and why you here?*"

By now, Ellen had stopped just outside the porch's screen door.

Ellen said, "I'm Ellen, Mrs. Richard Sheppard. You're sick, and I came to visit you."

Franklin said, "Jessie Mae, open the door and let Miz Sheppard in. Then you run home to yo' mama."

Jessie Mae stood up, put the Frederick Douglass book on the packing crate, then walked to the screen door.

As the colored girl opened the screen door for Ellen, she asked Franklin, "You sure, Mr.—?"

"Don't you say my name, girl!"

As Ellen stepped onto Franklin's porch, Franklin continued saying to Jessie Mae, "Yeah, I sure. And don't you come back till Miz Sheppard car, it done go far, y'hear?"

Jessie Mae said, "Miz Sheppard, she on yo' porch. You sure you wants me—?"

"Get on home, girl! But don't you worry none, I gone be fine."

Jessie Mae opened the screen door and let it slam itself shut, as the child ran away.

Ellen said, "She's gone."

Franklin said, "I think whatever you gots to say, no little child need to hear it."

"I brought you some food."

Franklin said, "That very white of you." After a pause, he asked, "Where it at?"

Franklin put his hands up, palms upturned. His hands were too far apart for the casserole dish.

Ellen put the casserole dish onto one of his upturned hands, making sure that her skin didn't brush against his.

But the casserole dish wobbled.

Franklin's other hand moved to grab the casserole dish from above.

Ellen panicked, because she didn't want this colored man touching her, even accidentally. She yanked the casserole dish away from him.

Ellen said, "I, *ahem*, see a crate with a book on it. I'll put this atop the book."

When Ellen had done that, Franklin said, "Have a seat, Miz Sheppard. Then you cans tell me, why you *really* here."

"Can't we please go inside?"

"A white woman with a barrel up yo' dress? Be I a fool?"

Ellen went to the "unoccupied" crate and dropped down ungracefully (due to her advanced pregnancy).

That unladylike behavior wasn't the worst part. Ellen couldn't shake the thought, *Any white person who drives by will see me at this colored man's house.*

****

In the kitchen of Johnny's farmhouse

A hand-cranked siren was started up in the watchtower, as Johnny slammed the earpiece back into the phone cradle. Carol rushed to the window to see what was going on.

Johnny turned to the woman who was cooking at the stove. "Betsy, take Carol and both y'all hide in the tornado shelter."

Everyone in the kitchen heard a gunshot.

Betsy said, "These men are killers?"

Outside, two of Johnny's men ran past the kitchen. Both men carried firearms.

Johnny said to Betsy and Carol, "Follow me. Make sure they don't see y'all."

Another shot was heard. A tommy-gun burst answered.

While Betsy grabbed Carol, Johnny grabbed the bayonet from under the kitchen table, before rushing out the kitchen door.

Behind Johnny, Betsy rushed Carol out the kitchen door. *Poor kid*, thought Johnny, *I'll bet she's scared to death.*

****

Meanwhile, on a dirt road near the farm

John Frost was driving a loaded truck marked "Frost's Hardware." John stopped when he heard the distant sound of the hand-cranked siren, followed by a gunshot.

He said, "What the hell?"

He heard another gunshot, followed by a tommy-gun burst.

He said, "That's Johnny's farm."

He quickly turned around the truck, to race back to town. John said, "Sheriff needs to know."

Chapter 29
Tension

Franklin's screened porch

Franklin glared at Ellen. "What you gots to tell me?"

Ellen said, "I care for you in Christ Jesus."

"No shit. Tell me, What be my name?"

Ellen said, "Franklin."

"*No*, girl. What be my *last* name?"

Ellen sighed. "I don't know."

Franklin said, "Mrs. Ellen Mary Frost Sheppard, may I present Mr. Franklin Basilius Hannah."

Ellen asked, "How do you know my middle name, Fr— Mister Hannah?"

Franklin said, "I be good with names and figures. You don't expect that from no nigger, sure enough."

****

The tornado shelter at Johnny's farm

The sounds of gunfire could be heard throughout.

The table and chairs were pushed away from one wooden wall, which was hinged at the top. Johnny was holding the fake wall up and away so that Betsy and Carol could get behind it.

In the dirt wall behind the fake wooden wall was a hole: only knee-high, but wide enough and deep enough for three adults lying on stomachs.

The hole held two tommy guns and a handgun. After Betsy and Carol scrambled into the hole—

Johnny said, "Betsy, I need one."

Betsy shoved out one tommy gun. Johnny let the fake wall swing closed, shoved the table and chairs against it, then picked up the tommy gun.

****

Franklin's screened porch

Upset Ellen was standing in a corner of the porch, arms folded as Franklin glared at her.

Ellen asked, "Why are you so angry at life, Mr. Hannah?"

"Because I be as smart as any white lawyer or banker, but all I be let do is haul ice."

"*Somebody* has to haul it."

Franklin said, "Not since white folk, they done been buying refrigerators. You thinks you knows so much? You ever hears of a man, Jabez McDaniel?"

Ellen was puzzled. The name wasn't familiar, and yet it was, almost. Ellen shook her head.

****

Johnny's farm

The battle was on. At the siren, Johnny's men had appeared, bearing serious firearms. Both sides were using WWI-surplus grenades. (One such grenade killed the tower guard.)

Johnny was personally responsible for five kills.

****

Franklin's screened porch

Franklin said, "Jabez McDaniel, he be running a whorehouse in Dallas. Won't let no colored boys in. But I hears he gots the finest white girls you ever be seeing— chained to they beds."

Ellen said, "The rumor is true? How *awful*."

"`How awful,' white women be slaves. *My* people, they done been in chains fo' hundreds of years. White church still ain't done say shit."

Ellen said, "But the white church is not Jesus. Don't be angry with God."

"You hush. If you ain't colored, you can't understand no anger."

Ellen snapped, "*Wrong*. If you haven't been raped, *you* can't understand anger."

Ellen made herself calm down. "But Jesus calls us to forgive those who wronged us."

****

Johnny's farm

Richard peeked around the corner of the farmhouse at the tornado shelter; he saw nobody alive.

Richard crept up to the tornado shelter, alert for danger.

He threw open the tornado-shelter doors.

****

In the hidey-hole in the tornado shelter

When Carol heard the sound of the tornado-shelter doors thrown open, she gasped.

Betsy shushed Carol and hugged her tightly.

Chapter 30
Deaths

The farmhouse and tornado shelter

Richard, peering into the tornado shelter, didn't notice Johnny behind him. Johnny had laid down his tommy gun and was sneaking up with the bayonet—he wanted to kill the traitor with his own hands.

Johnny grabbed Richard's hair, pulled him up, disemboweled him from behind, and cast him aside. Richard died managing to "speak" only a loud gasp.

Then Johnny saw Jabez trying to sneak up on him. Where Johnny was standing, if he looked through the window on the side of the farmhouse, he could also see through the window on the front of the farmhouse. Through those two windows, Johnny saw Jabez carrying a tommy gun and moving toward the corner of the building.

In response, Johnny dropped the bayonet and dived for his tommy gun. He picked it up and aimed it where he expected Jabez to appear.

****

Johnny was an instant too slow.

Jabez shot Johnny eight times, using the corner of the farmhouse as cover. Jabez smiled as he watched Johnny die.

Jabez, his gun smoking, then came around the corner to approach the bodies of Richard and Johnny.

Jabez kicked Richard's corpse. "I would've killed you if he hadn't."

Around the other side of the farmhouse came a man in overalls with a tommy gun. When he saw Jabez, he started firing. Jabez ducked into the shelter's stairwell and returned fire.

****

In the hidey-hole in the tornado shelter

The burst of fire from the submachine gun was deafening. Betsy and Carol heard a man yell, "*Die, hayseed bastard.*"

Carol whimpered in her terror. Betsy picked up the handgun that was stashed in the hidey-hole.

****

Jabez thought he heard something in the tornado shelter. But then the man in overalls drew Jabez's attention again.

Jabez said, "If I was that fella, I'd toss a hundred grenades into this hole."

Jabez fired a burst with his tommy gun. "Maybe he *can't*. Maybe it's a hideout."

Jabez fired a second burst with the tommy gun. "I haven't seen any women here. Maybe they're down there."

Jabez fired a third burst. "My whorehouse can use fresh faces."

The man in overalls tried a zigzag run toward the shelter stairs. He almost made it.

Jabez stopped to listen. All fighting was over, so Jabez heard nothing but the sounds of nature, and maybe—

****

In the hidey-hole in the tornado shelter

Carol was crying.

Frightened Betsy had a hand over Carol's mouth to mute her sobs. Betsy's other hand still gripped the gun.

****

In the tornado shelter

Jabez came down the steps into the tornado shelter. He went up to a wall; he pounded it with his fists and kicked it at the base. Both when pounded and kicked, the wall sounded solid.

Jabez remarked, "If the women have been fucking Johnny, I'll enjoy owning them."

Jabez went around two more walls—Jabez pounded and kicked on the walls, which sounded solid.

****

In the hidey-hole in the tornado shelter

Betsy and Carol were terrified.

Betsy got ready to shoot.

Chapter 31
Franklin's Challenge

Jabez stepped up to the fourth wall, about to test it.

Joe shouted from aboveground, "*Boss, you down here?*"

Jabez said, "What's up?"

Joe came down the tornado-shelter stairs. "Johnny and all his men are dead. We have only me, you, Freddy, and Dave. Do you want us to grab Johnny's stuff?"

Jabez shook his head. "Not enough fellas, not enough time. We got to run back to Dallas before the law shows up."

Jabez pounded the fourth wall once with his fists; the wall sounded solid. Jabez headed up the stairs with Joe.

****

Jabez and Joe came up the stairs. Jabez bent down to pick up Johnny's bloody bayonet, and pointed to Johnny's body with it. "Pick that fella up and take him back to the cars."

Joe said, "He's covered with blood."

"Don't give me lip."

****

Thirty seconds later
By Jabez's cars

Hoodlums Freddy and Dave, both injured, watched as Joe dropped Johnny to the ground.

Jabez, still holding the bayonet, knelt down by Johnny's corpse. "Watch and learn, boys."

What Jabez was doing shocked and revolted his men.

Jabez didn't give a rat. If people who heard the story treated Jabez with proper respect afterward, he figured he was ahead.

When Jabez finished his task, he gestured with the blood-covered bayonet. "Pass the word: I get angry when I'm messed with."

****

Meanwhile, on Franklin's screened porch

Franklin asked, "And you done forgive the man who done forced hisself on you?"

Ellen said, "I've asked God for strength—"

Franklin said, "Yeah, that so white. You tells the colored man do what you not do yo' ownself."

Ellen said, "If I'm so white, why am I here? Because Jesus said, `Visit the sick.' You think I want to be near a damn ni— Negro who's done nothing but holler at me?"

Franklin glared at Ellen. "You one of the folk who done burn the cross last night?"

He stood up. "When you forgives the man who done took you, then you comes talk to me about I forgives white folk."

Franklin felt his way to his house door and went inside his house. And either he'd forgotten about Ellen's casserole, or he had no interest in bringing it inside.

Ellen was shocked at Franklin's rude treatment of her.

Then she was angry. Then she felt torn.

****

Ten minutes later

Ellen's car was approaching Johnny's farm. She saw something to make her stop the car, step out, and look ahead.

Ellen said, "*No. Dear Jesus, please no.*"

Chapter 32
Baseball-Sized Hole

Ellen's car was approaching Johnny's farm. She saw something to make her stop the car, step out, and look ahead.

Ellen said, "*No. Dear Jesus, please no.*"

****

What Ellen saw—

• Many vultures circled overhead.

• At the entrance to the farm were five unexpected vehicles: an ambulance, a hearse, Sheriff Don's car, a car she'd never seen before (abandoned), and a fire truck.

• A deputy was directing a farmer with a team of horses, in towing away the abandoned car (which had no tags).

• Two men put a corpse into the hearse, closed the doors, then went back for more.

****

Two minutes later

Ellen was yelling, "Johnny? Carol? *Answer me!*"

Ellen, keyed up, was searching the grounds.

Unsuccessfully.

****

What Ellen saw as she searched—

• Corpses of moonshiners and men in suits were everywhere.

• One corpse, near the road entrance, was covered with a blood-soaked bedsheet.

• Plenty of ravens and crows watched everything.

• Firemen rolled up their hoses; half the barn was burned away.

****

As Ellen Sheppard continued to search for Johnny and Carol, the calls of the ravens and crows were loud, many, and nonstop. The carrion birds' racket made Sheriff Don's bad mood worse.

Sheriff Don stopped directing a photographer (who was taking a picture of a dead hoodlum), in order to move to and stop Ellen. Sheriff Don was sick with remorse, but knew he had a job to do.

Once he was within three feet of Ellen, he spoke formally: "Mrs. Sheppard, I need you to identify two bodies."

Ellen asked, "Where's Carol?"

The question confused him. He replied, "Found only men here. All dead."

****

Ellen realized Johnny and everyone she knew here was dead. Except maybe—

Ellen asked, "No sign of Betsy the cook either?"

When Sheriff Don shook his head, Ellen said, "Then either they're kidnapped, or they're hiding in the shelter, scared to death."

Sheriff Don replied, "Shelter's been checked."

"Did you look behind the fake wall?"

At Sheriff Don's look of surprise, Ellen moved toward the tornado shelter. But Sheriff Don grabbed her arm.

He pulled Ellen over toward the sheet-covered corpse.

After a glance back at the tornado shelter, Ellen let herself be led.

Sheriff Don said, "You don't want Carol to see her daddy's corpse—"

Ellen gasped. "Richard died in the raid?"

"He came here with gangsters, not Feds."

"Impossi—"

Sheriff Don said, "Now, you *really* don't want your girl to see Johnny here."

"Johnny took many gunshots?"

"Gunshots aren't the problem."

Sheriff Don and Ellen came up on the sheet-covered corpse. A crow was hopping around, trying to figure out how to get to the food underneath.

Sheriff Don jerked his gun from his holster and shot the crow. Ellen felt alarmed as Sheriff Don reholstered his gun.

Sheriff Don growled, "Cocksucking crows."

He pulled the sheet away. Ellen was horrified.

The sheriff's voice got formal: "Is this the body of Horace John Carter?"

Ellen said, "*Johnny?* My sweet Johnny?"

****

What Ellen saw—

Johnny's shirt had been ripped apart, exposing his chest and abdomen. His naked chest had three bullet holes in it, but that wasn't the worst part.

Just below Johnny's breastbone was a baseball-sized opening that was filled with blood. A human heart laid on the ground, inches from the body.

Johnny's bayonet laid next to him. Most of the blade was painted red with blood.

****

Sheriff Don said, "Crows were chewing on the heart when I got here."

He covered up Johnny's corpse—and furious Ellen was waiting for him when he looked up.

"How much were you paid to allow this?" she demanded.

"Stop, I feel bad enou—"

Ellen said, "Spare me your crap."

"Dammit, our deal was meant to be *fun*—Johnny makes money, I make money, everybody wins."

****

Minutes later
By the tornado shelter

Carol was clutching Ellen as Betsy talked to Sheriff Don. Ellen listened to Betsy while soothing Carol.

Betsy told Sheriff Don, "Johnny said, `It's Jabez!' That's all I know."

Ellen said, "Then his full name might be Jabez McDaniel, he might run a bawdy house in Dallas—*wait*."

Now Ellen realized why that name sounded familiar. She scooped up Carol and rushed to her car.

Sheriff Don asked, "Where you going? Where'd you get this Jabez fella's last name?"

Ellen called back, "From a colored man with a great memory. Gotta go!"

****

One minute later

Ellen stuffed Carol into the passenger seat of the car, hurried around to the driver's side, and started the car. The car rushed past a roadside sign sequence:

Love your enemies
Bless them
Do good to them
And pray for them
Matt. 5:44

****

A half-hour later
Brother Bob's church office

Brother Bob was writing a sermon when Ellen rushed in.

Ellen rushed past the wall-mounted telephone and up to Brother Bob's desk. "I need a book about people of the Bible."

Without waiting for permission, Ellen moved to Brother Bob's bookshelves, found such a book, yanked it off the shelf, and flipped pages.

Brother Bob said, "Your aunt and uncle lost their son. Why aren't you comforting them?"

Ellen said in a flat voice, "Jabez, Jabez, Ja—*Jabez*. When I see Uncle Horace, I want to give words of *true* comfort. `And his mother—' "

Brother Bob wasn't annoyed now, he's horrified. "Murder doesn't fit you."

Ellen said, "If the same man who cut up Johnny like a dead pig, also *shamed* me? You'd be amazed what fits me."

Brother Bob said, "If you know Johnny's killer, God forbids you to kill him. `Vengeance is mine; I will repay, saith the Lord.' "

Ellen said, "'And his mother called his name Jabez, saying, Because I bare him with sorrow.' You circled *Jabez* and wrote *pain* in the margin—why?"

Brother Bob said, "For someone who pledged to copy Jesus, you're acting more unchristian than ever."

Ellen demanded, "Why write *pain* about Jabez?"

Brother Bob replied, "*Yabets* means sorrow, pain, or affliction. Whatev—"

Ellen looked off into the distance. "Jabez McDaniel, Daniel Payne, Danny Payne—it fits."

Ellen shut the book, and slapped it down onto Brother Bob's desk. "*Me*, unchristian? When's the last time you were inside Colored Town or any jail?"

"Too long, I admit. But take my advice—"

Ellen said, "*No.* I took your advice about Prohibition. But Johnny and Richard are dead because of Prohibition, and my rapist grows rich."

Ellen walked to the door.

Before she left, Brother Bob said, "Listen, hatred corrodes your soul. God commanded 'Forgive your enemy' for *your* sake, not his."

Ellen said, "Bob, how did making laws become more important to us Christians than saving souls? What a mess I helped make."

With that, she left.

Contrite Brother Bob went to his knees. "Lord, my sins have found me out. She won't listen to me."

Chapter 33
Ellen Sins, And Sins Again

That night
In the living room of Ellen's parents' house

Near the front door, Dad and Mommy worried, and Carol wailed. Ellen was dressed to travel. Carol hugged her mother with all her strength.

Carol was crying a river. "Don't leave me, mommy!"

Ellen said, "I have to go, cupcake. Mommy has to talk to Daddy's boss tomorrow morning."

Dad said, "Why not tomorrow afternoon? Only a fool goes motoring when temperature's this close to freezing."

Mommy said, "Your car will break down, in the cold, in the dark, miles from—"

The phone rang in the kitchen. Mommy dashed off.

Dad asked, "What's the *real* reason you're rushing to Dallas now?"

Ellen replied, "I told you. I have a 9 a.m. appointment with Mr. Wainwright."

Dad looked skeptical (and rightly so), but before he could say more—

Mommy called from the kitchen, "Ellen, it's Brother Bob. Says it's urgent!"

****

Ellen said, "Make it brief, Brother Bob. I'm fixing to motor to Dallas."

Brother Bob said, "You have plans for Jabez."

"*Oh,* yes."

"Sister Ellen, consider Jesus' last day on earth. Judas betrayed him, the Jewish leaders plotted to kill him, the Roman soldiers did kill him, and Pontius Pilate allowed him to die."

"Make your point."

Brother Bob said, "Yet what did Jesus say in his agony? `Father, forgive them: for they know not what they do.' "

"Jesus also said, `My God, my God, why hast thou forsaken me?' "

Ellen hung up on Brother Bob.

****

In the living room of John and Audrey Frost's house

John and Audrey were playing with Carol. Ellen walked in from the kitchen and took John aside. This fed John's suspicions.

Ellen said, "If anything happens, make sure Carol gets love, okay?"

John asked, "What might happen?"

"I could get killed in a traffic accident."

John grabbed Ellen's shoulders. "Why are you leaving? I want truth."

Ellen looked into her father's eyes. "What do you think of a man who drugs a girl, then violates her?"

"You don't trust me? You couldn't tell me before?"

Ellen said, "I love you, Dad. I love Mommy and I love Carol—tell them."

****

Twenty minutes later
Johnny's farm at night

Betsy and the hearses, ambulances, wagons, corpses, and crows all were long gone; Johnny's property was deserted except for Ellen's car.

No light came from house or barn. The car's engine was running, and the headlights shined on the stairs of the tornado shelter.

Ellen came up the stairs, closed the shelter doors, and walked to the driver's-side door. Ellen carried the handgun that she had found in the hidey-hole behind the fake wall.

With each step from the tornado shelter to the car door, Ellen moved farther out of the path lit by the headlights. Ellen became a dim, then dark, figure.

Ellen thought, *I want it this way. Walking in the light is overrated.*

PART 3
What Matters Prohibition In Eternity?

Chapter 34
Talking With Road Signs

One hour later at night

Ellen was traveling a dirt road, the handgun laying on the passenger seat. Ellen passed a roadside sign series:

Father, forgive them
For they know not
What they do.
Luke 23:34

Ellen wasn't buying. "But Jesus, when you hung on the cross, didn't part of you wish lions would rip Judas' legs off?"

Another roadside series:

But if ye forgive not
Men their trespasses
Neither will your Father
Forgive your trespasses.
Matt. 6:15

Ellen glared at stars. "You'll burn me in hell because I don't like being drugged and raped?"

Be not overcome
Of evil
But overcome evil
With good.
Rom. 12:21

Ellen said, "Forget it. I won't walk any second mile or turn the other cheek, not for Jabez."

Lord, how oft
Shall I forgive him?
Seven times?
Jesus saith unto him,
Seventy times seven.
Matt. 18:21-22

Ellen said, "Forgiving Jabez *once* is impossible."

With God
All things
Are possible.
Mark 10:27

Ellen was no longer blindly furious, but she was still angry. "Why am I even in this mess? I'm not a bad person, Lord, I don't deserve this."

All things work
Together for good
To them that love God.
Rom. 8:28

Ellen said, "*Yeah?* Jabez is twice rich now, from both white slavery and bootlegging. How does that work for good?"

Be not deceived
God is not mocked.
What a man soweth
Shall he reap
Gal. 6:7

Ellen said, "But reap on Judgment Day. I want Jabez to suffer *now*."

The arms of the wicked
Shall be broken

But the Lord
Upholdeth the righteous.
Ps. 37:17

Ellen said, "When you break Danny Payne's arms, can I watch?"

She was no longer angry. She was calm enough now that she could smile at her own joke.

She said, "I feel better, talking to you."

My peace
I give unto you
Let not your
Heart be troubled.
John 14:27

Ellen said, "I give Jabez to you, Lord. But part of me still wants to kill him."

Ellen passed one more roadside series:

If we confess our sins
He is faithful
To forgive
And to cleanse us
from unrighteousness.
1 John 1:9

****

The Texas countryside at night

Ellen stopped the car, but let the engine idle. She started to leave the car, then grabbed the handgun. Ellen walked just in front of a headlight.

Any farmhouses nearby were dark, and no other vehicles traveled this road now. Except for the moon, the stars, and the car's headlights, all was darkness.

But Ellen stood in light.

The only sounds were night insects and the idling car engine.

Ellen looked at the gun for a second, feeling torn—then she hurled the gun away. She turned to face the car, then fell to her knees, ashamed and repentant.

"I'm so wicked, Lord. I lusted in my heart for Johnny, and all this ruin comes from that. Richard turned jealous enough to kill, because of my lust. Johnny died without Jesus, because of my lust. I've neglected Carol to make this trip to kill Jabez, whom I hated with an unforgiving heart. Lord Jesus, I am a vile, sinful woman. Forgive me. Amen."

****

Ellen pulled herself up to stand, returned to the driver's seat, and resumed her driving. For a time she was silent, thoughtful. Then she slammed on the brakes. After the car had stopped—

"Lord, I forgive Jabez McDaniel for his sins against me. Amen."

Ellen put her foot on the gas and the car moved forward again.

"But he still must be stopped," Ellen told God.

Chapter 35
Rescuing The Captives

The next morning
On a Dallas street

Very pregnant Ellen stood at the curb by a taxi, trying to persuade the taxi driver to take her to Jabez's brothel.

Ellen's skirt was wet in places, clinging to her legs, but Ellen ignored that.

Now the taxi driver said, "I won't help you pull your husband out, ma'am."

Ellen said, "It's the *girls* I intend to drag out, not any man."

"You got a derringer in your purse? A knife?"

Ellen smiled. "I'm unarmed."

The taxi driver said, "What if he slaps those chains on you? I'm not gonna help you."

Ellen nodded. "Understood."

"In fact, you pay me off before you go in. I won't wait for you."

Ellen began, "Okay. . ."

Ellen went rigid with a labor contraction. When she could speak again, she said, ". . .with me."

The taxi driver eyed the wet blotches on Ellen's skirt. "Ma'am, you need to go to—"

"Jabez McDaniel's brothel. Hurry—today is a busy day."

With difficulty Ellen got into the back seat, and the taxi drove away.

From the back seat, Ellen said, "Driver, do you know Jesus forgives sins? And I ought to know."

****

Ten minutes later
Jabez's brothel

Joe was sitting in a chair in the lower floor of the brothel, and he was bored silly.

Because of the shootout, the brothel was understaffed: Lucas the brothel cashier had no exclusive armed guard, and Joe had to be bouncer both for upstairs and downstairs.

A very pregnant woman walked into the brothel. Joe figured this respectable woman had walked in by mistake. Joe saw Lucas frown; Joe figured Lucas wanted the pregnant woman quickly gone.

Joe at first took no interest in the conversation between Lucas and the pregnant woman.

****

Ellen was energized. She was at peace with herself, at peace with God, and she felt rock-solid assurance that the Lord of Hosts supported her mission. She was determined to complete this mission, despite going into labor.

The cashier asked, "Where are you trying to go, ma'am?"

Contraction! When it passed—

Ellen asked, "Is this the bawdy house of Jabez McDaniel?"

The cashier said, "Yes—I mean no, we're a hotel. But we have no vacancies."

Ellen pointed at him, and loudly she quoted Scripture: " `Depart from me, all ye workers of iniquity; for the Lord hath heard the voice of my weeping.' "

The cashier looked unnerved, and glanced at a bored-looking big man at the other end of the hallway.

The cashier said, "Ma'am, it's *you* who will have to—"

Ellen proclaimed, "'The Lord shall send upon thee cursing, vexation, and rebuke, because of the wickedness of thy doings.' Minion of Jabez McDaniel, begone."

Ellen's total confidence and her Bible quotes frightened the cashier, and he fled out the front door, leaving the cashier-cage door wide open.

****

The pregnant lady had walked in, and had spoken briefly with Lucas, and Joe had expected her to hurry out the front door. Instead, she had pointed at Lucas, loudly quoted Bible stuff, and it was *Lucas* who had run out the front door.

In the process, leaving the cashier-cage door open!

This brought Joe rushing up, gun drawn, as the pregnant woman called out to fleeing Lucas, "Confess your sins and give your life to Jesus—let Him save you."

Joe said, "Whoever you are, lady, leave now."

The woman eyed Joe's gun. Joe expected to see fear then. Instead, with the confidence of a queen, she put her hand out: *Give me.*

She quoted the Bible again, this time to Joe: "'Now hear me therefore, and deliver the captives: for the fierce wrath of the Lord is upon you.'"

"Who *are* you?"

"Jabez knew me as Ellen. I knew *him* as Danny Payne."

Joe stared. "You're the girl who got away?"

Ellen said, "Yes. Your gun and your keys, please."

Though Joe was much bigger than Ellen, now he felt fear of her. He pointed his gun at her. "You're crazy!"

Ellen said, "'For behold, the Lord will come with fire, and with his chariots like a whirlwind, to render his anger with fury, and his rebuke with flames of fire.' Your gun and your keys, please."

Joe was as spooked as Lucas. Joe shoved his gun at Ellen, yanked the key-ring from his pocket and dropped it to the floor, and bolted.

Ellen yelled to his retreating back, "Accept Jesus as Lord and ask His forgiveness—let Him save you."

****

One minute later
Jabez's brothel, Room 11

An old man, naked, was enjoying the room's gaunt, chained girl when Ellen walked in. Ellen was at the end of a contraction.

The old man said, "What the hell?"

Ellen panted, "Stop. Dress. Go."

"Not till I get my money's worth."

Ellen gave him a small smile. "I have labor pains, and a gun. Hm?"

The old man rushed to dress as Room 11's girl cowered. When the man was dressed—

Ellen said, "Ask Jesus to forgive you, and make Him your Lord—let Him save you."

The old man looked at Ellen as if she were crazy, then rushed out the door.

Ellen went to the chained girl, who clearly was terrified of her.

Ellen said, "Honey, I'm here to rescue you."

Ellen tried to find the key on the guard's ring for the padlock at the girl's neck. While Ellen tried keys—

The girl asked, "How far apart, your contractions?"

"A minute."

The girl said, "If Mr. McDaniel catches you, you're in trouble."

Ellen said, "If he *doesn't* catch me, I'm in labor. Life is good."

No luck with the keys. Ellen gestured for the girl to move far away from the bed. The girl stretched the chain taut.

Ellen said, "I saw this in the flickers." She aimed the guard's gun at where the chain attached to the bedpost.

Blam!

Just missed. The bullet gouged a hole in the floor.

The girl said, "Now Mr. McDaniel will come for sure."

"I don't think he's here."

Blam! Missed again. *Blam!* The chain was cut from the bedpost.

"I'm *free*," the girl said, in a voice filled with wonder. "I'm human again."

Ellen said, "Leave here now, honey. Telephone the newspaper, *then* telephone the police. And then—"

"Yes?"

Ellen said, "Give your life to Jesus and ask Him to forgive your sins."

****

One minute later
Jabez's brothel, Room 15

Millie and her customer were sitting up in bed, all thoughts of sex forgotten. They heard a man's footsteps running down the hall, then a gunshot from Room 13. After several seconds, they heard another gunshot from Room 13. Soon thereafter, Millie and her customer heard a woman's footsteps running, the rattle of chains, and the joyful voice of a young woman yelling—

"Rot in hell, broke-dicks. I faked it every time."

Millie's customer tried to put his arm around Millie. She shoved him away.

A woman's footsteps walked to the room door, the door opened, and a pregnant woman entered—with the smoking gun in her hand.

The pregnant woman obviously was suffering. Millie would have bet money (if she'd had money to bet), that the gunwoman was already dilated.

Millie's customer asked, "You here to kill us?"

"I'm here to stop you from further sin."

The man dashed naked out the door, before the pregnant woman could say another word.

As the pregnant woman gestured Millie off the bed and aimed at the chain, the woman said, "Don't know how much time I have."

"Till McDaniel shows up?" Millie asked.

"That too."

Blam! But one chain-link was only cracked, not cut clean away. The woman aimed again. *Click*—empty gun.

Millie said, "Shit. I'll have to work it apart."

As Millie squatted and worked on the chain, the pregnant woman tossed the gun on the bed. Then, with obvious relief, she sat on the bed herself.

The woman sighed. "I'm sorry, I can't help you now."

Millie said, "Hurry, *leave*. Why you being an idiot, anyway?"

"Because Jesus would."

Millie felt scorn—this woman clearly didn't know the real world.

Millie pulled the chain free from the damaged link. Too emotional to speak, Millie held it up for the pregnant woman to see.

Chapter 36
Pain And Payne

Jabez's brothel, top of the stairs

Ellen and the Room 15 girl were at the top of the stairs. Ellen said, through another contraction, "Get out of here *now*, before—"

"Too late," a man's voice said. Ellen had not heard that voice since 1916, but she recognized it.

Jabez, gun drawn, raced up the stairs. But while Ellen was in agony, she was not frightened.

Jabez/Danny was a little thicker in the waist in 1924, and his face had deeper lines. His face showed no sign of the attractive smile that 1916 Danny had charmed Ellen with.

Ellen said to him, "Two escaped. The police are coming."

"Maybe. Think you'll live to know? Millie, back to your room."

With a gun pointed at her, Millie didn't argue. Ellen heard Millie's bare feet walk to Room 15 and shut the door.

Jabez asked, "Do you know what happened to Joe?"

Ellen said, "Is he the cashier, or the guard?"

"When he told me he gave his gun to a woman, I shot him *twice*."

Ellen said, "In Jesus I forgive you for all you've done."

"Ain't you sweet. I killed your cousin Johnny and ripped out his ticker. *Now* what do you say?"

Ellen was serene. "You also raped me, besides trying to make me one of these girls. I still forgive you."

Jabez zipped forward, to press Ellen against the upstairs railing. This put his back to the upstairs rooms. He said, "I could push you over this railing *so* easy. Maybe you'd live. The brat wouldn't."

Ellen said, "Jesus died for your sins."

"*Stop* with that shit. You want everyone to think you're sweet and good because you pop out babies? Bullshit."

"Your mother must have really hurt you."

Jabez slapped Ellen with his free hand. Anger surged in Ellen for an instant, but she calmed herself.

Jabez now pasted on an amused smile. "Tell me, do you forgive your husband?"

"For taking up with you? Yes."

Jabez said, "You dumb Dora. Richard had sex with Millie and two other girls here. Millie gave him a blowjob—something you've never done, I'm told. *Still* forgive him?"

Ellen was rocked by this news, but soon she said, "Yes. As I forgive you, and urge you to give your life to Jesus and ask His forgiveness."

Jabez aimed his gun at Ellen's stomach. "Think your goody-goody act will stop me from killing you, your brat, and that bitch whore Millie?"

Ellen said, "No, it is *God* who'll stop you. `For God is able to deliver, and will deliver.' "

Ellen raised her voice: "*I urge you not to kill—murder is major sin.*"

Jabez grinned. "Haw, go ahead, beg for your life."

"I wasn't talking to *you*, but to *Millie*. Jabez, look out!"

Jabez's face showed scorn and skepticism—right up to the moment that Millie dropped her chain around his throat.

Ellen stepped forward, intending to help Jabez, but she got a surprise.

She felt a long and sharp pain—

No! Not now! Please, Lord, this is the wrong time!

—and from experience knew what that pain meant: Her cervix was dilating, she was giving birth!

Ellen couldn't stop from screaming.

Meanwhile, Jabez was waving the gun around, clearly with the idea of shooting Millie. But it was difficult to aim at someone he couldn't see behind him, and Ellen was sure that Jabez couldn't think clearly right then.

Ellen was rigid with pain, no help to Jabez. Ellen said between pants, "Girl, you should stop. . ."

As Ellen slumped to the floor—

****

—Jabez struggled for his life.

1) Jabez smashed against walls and doors, trying to knock Millie off.

2) But Millie wrapped her legs around his waist, and continued to strangle him.

3) Jabez's arm movements became less precise and controlled. He seemed close to losing consciousness.

4) But then Jabez put the gun barrel to Millie's head.

5) Millie threw her butt back, making her and Jabez fall backward.

6) While falling, Millie twisted her body to the right; she and Jabez fell on their right sides.

7) Caught by surprise, Jabez moved his gun hand to break his fall.

8) Instead, Jabez's right arm was pinned underneath.

9) Jabez couldn't free his arm, for by now he was barely conscious.

10) Millie's arms were free, and she used her whole body to finish strangling Jabez.

11) Jabez died, while Ellen was suffering pain of childbirth.

****

Millie stood up, then kicked the corpse. "Fucking prick bastard."

A door slammed downstairs, then a male voice yelled, *"This is the police!"*

Weak Ellen barely raised a hand above the upstairs railing. "Up here."

Ellen looked in Millie's eyes. In a weak voice, Ellen said, "You need to forgive. . ."

Chapter 37
Sunday Gathering Of Believers

Noon, that Sunday
First Baptist Church, Tateville

The service had just ended; church members were chatting on the lawn, and several parking places were vacant. A family twenty feet away from Brother Bob, they waved to a couple leaving by automobile. As Brother Bob was talking to John and Audrey Frost, old Mrs. Carter and old Widow Manx listened in.

Brother Bob asked, "And Sister Ellen? Are she and the baby out of the hospital?"

Audrey said, "Ellen and Billy returned to town yesterday. But Ellen had things to do today."

Mrs. Carter said, "Probably ashamed to show herself in church."

Widow Manx said, "She's no longer respectable, it's true."

Brother Bob heard an old truck drive up.

****

The Frost Hardware And Lumber truck pulled up and parked. As the church members gaped—

Woody got out of the driver door, and came around to the passenger side. Woody helped Ellen—baby Billy asleep on her shoulder—get out of the truck.

Ellen handed Woody a box of saltine crackers, a coffee cup, and an unlabeled bottle of murky wine.

Woody and Ellen went to the back of the truck and helped Millie, then Carol, then Franklin get down. With Ellen guiding Franklin, the six people headed into the church.

Millie looked awful: the poor woman was suffering heroin withdrawal.

Ellen saw Mrs. Carter angrily gesture for Brother Bob to come over.

When Brother Bob was standing near the old biddies, Widow Manx said, "That woman is bringing a colored man into our church."

Brother Bob shocked Ellen when he said, "And that's bad because. . .?"

Widow Manx said, "Hmph."

Ellen had something more important to do than to listen to those two women prattle. Ellen led her group into the now-empty Baptist church.

Brother Bob evidently was curious what Ellen was planning. He followed Ellen's group into the foyer of the church, then the two old biddies and other church members followed him.

****

The five people Ellen had brought all sat in the front pew; little Carol held baby Billy. Ellen walked the floor between the front pew and the pulpit. Franklin, Millie, Woody, and Carol all had heads bowed as Ellen held up a cracker.

Ellen quoted: " `. . .took bread, and gave thanks, and brake it, and gave unto them, saying, This is my body which is given for you: this do in remembrance of me.' "

Ellen broke the cracker into four pieces. She gave a piece to everyone but the children. Solemnly, all four communicants ate their piece of cracker.

Ellen poured wine into the coffee cup, which she raised.

Ellen quoted more Scripture: " `Likewise also the cup after supper, saying, This cup is the new testament in my blood, which is shed for you.' "

Before Ellen could do anything with the cup, one of the old biddies spoke loudly—

Widow Manx said, "Brother Bob, *do* something. That woman killed a man in Dallas. She was in the paper."

Millie said, "Gracious, I should leave."

Church members murmured, but Ellen was calm—

Ellen said, "The District Attorney dropped charges. And Millie has given her life to Jesus, asking His forgiveness."

Ellen saw Widow Manx looking daggers at Brother Bob. But Brother Bob said only, "These three with you who ate the cracker: Are they baptized?"

Ellen grinned. "Yesterday, in the Leon River. Dad wore his waders. I had towels ready. It was *cold* outside."

Brother Bob nodded, and said nothing more.

Mrs. Carter said, "This all is *blasphemy!* Brother Bob, stop this! Up there she has a nigger, a murderess, and a bootlegger, and she's holding communion with bootleg wine!"

Ellen said, "It's what Jesus would do."

Ellen sipped from the coffee cup, then passed it to Franklin.

THE END

If you liked this story: **Please go to its Amazon page and write a five-star review. Thank you.**